Nightmare in Pewter

Nightmare in Pewter

JEAN DEWEESE

DOUBLEDAY & COMPANY, INC.

GARDEN CITY, NEW YORK

1978

All of the characters in this book are fictitious,
and any resemblance to actual persons, living or
dead, is purely coincidental.

ISBN: 0-385-12097-4
Library of Congress Catalog Card Number 78–3257
Copyright © 1978 by Gene DeWeese
All Rights Reserved
Printed in the United States of America
First Edition

For the Fulton County (Indiana) Historical Society, especially for its pleasantly pushy president, Shirley Willard.

Nightmare in Pewter

She awakened once again, screaming silently in her mind, trying desperately to drown out the voice, to somehow halt the insane words that stabbed at her endlessly out of nowhere.

The bedroom curtains still billowed gently in the breeze, but the air had turned cold and chilling, and the gooseflesh that it raised on her bare arms and shoulders intensified the horror of the soundless, unstoppable assault. Lurching into a sitting position on the side of the bed, she grasped the window and slammed it down with a force that rattled the counterweights, as if violent physical action could force the voice out of her brain.

But it did not. There was no way she could escape. She knew that now. After a half dozen nights of futile, terrified resistance, of doctors and pills and crying, she knew at last that there was nothing she could do but endure as she waited for another dawn.

On the first night, the voice had been distant and indistinct, like someone far out on the lake; but each night it came closer, and each night she slept less. Each night, she knew that insanity was driving its wedge deeper and deeper into her mind. Each night, after increasingly desperate efforts to close out the imagined sounds, she lay staring fearfully into the darkness, waiting for the inevitable appearance of whatever creature her mind would choose to manufacture as a source for the voice.

For that was how it worked. She couldn't remember the name for her illness, but she knew that that was how it worked, how it progressed. First were the auditory hallucinations, then the visual. In the end, the hallucinations would enfold her, and the last remnants of the real world would fade from sight. She shuddered at the thought of such total loss of control over her own mind and body, but she knew it was coming. She knew.

And she knew that, during the nights, there was even now no

way to escape it. No matter which way she turned, no matter how deeply she buried her head beneath the covers and pillows, the alien thing within her mind kept up its incessant clamor. There was no escape but sleep, and sleep was rapidly becoming impossible. Each night, the effect of the pills became less and less. Each night, she came awake earlier and more often. Each night, the dawn seemed farther and farther away.

She forced herself to lie still, forced herself to breathe slowly and regularly, forced herself to close her eyes and think, over and over, setting up a counterrhythm to the unceasing repetitions of the voice:

"Soon it will be dawn. Soon it will be dawn. Soon it will be dawn . . ."

CHAPTER 1

Shelbie Wilson looked up from the litter of government forms she had been struggling with, past the half dozen shadowy, glass-topped display cases along the wall to her right, and through the broad archway into the next, cavernous room. The square, multi-paned windows set high in the wall to her left reflected only the cold fluorescent glow that filtered up from the drafting lamp clamped to the edge of her desk. The papers rustled as she shifted her hands on the desktop, and the sounds seemed to be amplified by the surrounding silence and the echoes from the bare concrete floors and high, girdered ceilings. The only evidence that the outside world still existed was a distant, muffled rumble that might have been the engine of a semi pulling away from the stoplight on Main, nearly two blocks away.

And that was all. Beyond those few, faint sounds, beyond the small island of light centered on her desk, there was only darkness and silence.

And yet there was something—something that had prompted her to look up . . .

Shelbie blinked, shaking her head sharply, forcing herself to look down at the papers again, at the endless blanks in triplicate and quadruplicate. It was just the time of night that was getting to her, she told herself. Just the time and the location; that was all. As long as she could remember, school buildings at night had always seemed to be a world somehow divorced from reality. The rooms and halls, whether darkened and deserted or filled with parents and students at PTA meetings or class plays, were not the same rooms and halls that existed during the day. No matter how much light there was inside the building, no matter how many people were talking and laughing, there was always an awareness of the outer darkness that lay over the building and shrouded the grounds that surrounded it. The darkness seemed to seep in, touching the walls, the distant ceilings, the desks, the blackboards, touching and subtly altering everything in a way that could not be seen or heard but simply felt. Or perhaps, Shelbie had sometimes thought during her occasional uncharacteristically somber moods, it was not that the building changed at night but that she herself changed. Perhaps she carried a bit of that darkness within herself, allowing it to shade her surroundings, alter her reactions to things and to people. Even during her four years as a teacher, when it seemed that she had spent half her evenings directing and rehearsing school plays, the feeling had remained, often lending a certain unreality to the plays themselves, giving the whole affair a sense of drama that the plays did not warrant.

And now that this particular building—the one that had seen Shelbie through high school a decade before—was no longer even a school, but a collection of offices, clubs, meeting halls, and museums, the feeling was even stronger. There was the double unreality of the night and of the changes to the building itself. Where bare wooden floors and permanently mounted desks had once stood in rows, there were now thick blue carpets and couches and coffee tables. Where the files and desks of the principal's office had been, there were now the straight-back chairs and rounded tables of a senior citizens' bridge club. And where the benches and machines for shop classes had been, there were now the crowded exhibit cases and antique furniture and ancient farm equipment of the Farrell County Historical Society Museum.

Again Shelbie looked up from the papers, irritably wondering if the "feeling" that nagged at her so persistently was coming from the darkened rooms of the museum or from her own impatience with the forms she had been struggling with for far too many hours. Anything, her subconscious mind might be telling her, is preferable to another hour of trying to second-guess the bureaucrats who had designed the forms and would no doubt go over them in their own single-minded way when she had completed them and sent them in. *If* she ever completed them.

Annoyed—half at herself, half at the faceless people behind the forms—she stood up abruptly, running the fingers of both hands roughly through the loosely curling, short brown tangle that was her hair. She stood for a moment, looking at nothing, then swiveled the drafting lamp on its jointed metal arm until the fluorescent glow lit the far wall and poured through the arch and into the next room like a gigantic, diffuse flashlight. The desk, and herself behind it, were fully in shadow.

For another moment, she stood silently, listening and watching, but still there was nothing—as she had known there would be nothing. Just nerves, or an excuse to stand up for a minute. Or maybe even an excuse to knock off for the night and forget the whole mess until tomorrow. After all, the deadline for the completed forms was still a couple of days away, and there was no need to knock herself out tonight. Time enough for that tomorrow or the day after.

She walked around the desk, the rippled soles of her flats slapping against the concrete of the floor, the first real sound she had heard since standing up. At the broad arch into the next room, she stood for a moment looking into the shadows.

No sound. No motion.

There were only the relics, the artifacts. She could just make out the rusting, horse-drawn hay rake in one corner, the box wagon waiting to be restored in another, the small pieces of farm equipment arranged haphazardly around the rest of the room. And herself, the only thing in the room less than seventy years old—unless you counted the dimly glowing red exit sign over the metal door in the opposite wall. Tonight, though, she fit right in with the rest of the room. Her jeans, faded more from use than from style or fashion, would have been at home on any farm, as would the plain cardigan sweater she had pulled on over her blouse as the evening coolness had drifted into the as-yet-unheated building.

Shelbie turned back toward her desk, then grimaced as she caught a glimpse of herself in the glass-fronted cabinet behind the desk. She had the feeling that, if she had the nerve to look at the reflection more closely, she would find an uncomfortable amount of redness to contrast with the greenish-blue of her eyes. Even from this distance, in this faint light, she could see that her rounded, oval face appeared more than a little tired, maybe even haggard, and the hair, tangled rather than tousled, didn't help matters. And her whole body—including the dozen or so extra pounds she couldn't seem to ever get rid of—was slumping, making her look even shorter than her barely five-feet-plus.

Yes, she thought, it was definitely time to knock off for the night. For a practically nonpaying, "temporary" job, this burning of the midnight oil—or midnight fluorescents—was just a bit much. Doing it when she had been a teacher, having to keep up with grades and plays and themes, was one thing; but doing it now, for little more than the "honor" of being president of the Farrell County Historical Society, was something else. One of these days, she would definitely have to unload the job on someone else, the same way it had been unloaded on her by Marge Remington nearly a year before. Not that Shelbie could ever be quite as smooth about the unloading—or about anything else—as Marge had been, but she was learning. Since the society could pay for practically none of the work or material it needed, she was very definitely learning. If she hadn't been, she would have given up in sheer frustration after the first week. Trying to get money was—

Frowning, Shelbie turned sharply to her left, toward one of the long, glass-topped display cases that stood a couple of feet out from the wall. Had she heard something? Or was it just the inner rattling of her own thoughts?

Slowly, she moved toward the display case at the end of the row, half in the light from her desk lamp, half in shadow. On the floor at the shadowed end of the case, a two-foot-high wooden owl stared at her grotesquely, and she shivered as her eyes brushed across it. Who, she wondered, had donated *that* horror? And who had accepted it? She knew that people who were cleaning out their attics tended to bring the society anything and everything they couldn't sell anywhere else, but there ought to be some kind of standard for what they had to accept.

Then her eyes were drawn back to the display case, to the large brass clock with the greenish cherub poised precariously on its top, to the yellowing meerschaum carving next to it, to the photo album that lay open near one end of the case, to the windup phonograph complete with horn, to the disturbingly ugly little pewter head, to the—

She blinked as the feeling touched her once again. Her eyes darted in all directions: toward the display cases, toward the room behind her, even toward the windows and the shadowy ceiling a dozen feet above her. But of course there was nothing.

Abruptly, she strode back to her desk, a paper-littered island in the middle of the neatly arranged, table-height display cases. With quick, determined motions, she shuffled the forms loosely together into a stack, dumped the stack into a drawer, snatched up her purse from another drawer, turned off the drafting lamp, and hurried back into the larger room and toward the broad metal door leading to the alley back of the building. The red exit sign gave her just enough light to pick her way through the maze of ancient farm equipment.

Halfway through the room, she stopped. There was a sound, a metallic rattling. Not just a vague, insubstantial "feeling," but an actual sound.

But where? And what had—

It came again, and this time she pinpointed the source: the door to the alley, which was also the main entrance to the museum.

Uneasily, she looked around in the near darkness. At this time of night, with everything in the building closed down, there was no reason for anyone to be here. There wasn't even a good reason for being here herself, and if—

Involuntarily, Shelbie's mind darted back to the week before, when someone had come in to work one morning to find the door unlocked. Nothing had been disturbed as far as anyone could tell, and they finally decided that, no matter what their memories said, one of them must have left the door unlocked the night before. But still . . .

"Shelbie? Is that you?"

For a split second, she stiffened, her heart suddenly accelerating; but before the second was over, she recognized the voice, the distinctive combination of drawl and preciseness. Dick Reynolds, one of the sheriff's deputies, working nights this month.

"Yes, Dick, it's me," she said to the door, and a moment later it opened slowly, creakily. Sighing, she went the rest of the way across the room.

"Everything all right?" He stood holding the door open, playing the beam from a flashlight around the darkened room. Short and slender, but solid as the proverbial rock, boyish looking despite his thirty-odd years, he looked like a small-town version of Michael Sarazin, Shelbie had always thought. He snapped off the huge five-cell flashlight, and Shelbie's eyes quickly adjusted to the faint illumination that filtered in from a distant street lamp.

"Everything's fine," she said. "I've just been working a little late, that's all."

"A *little* late?" He grinned, somehow managing to look even younger than he already did—certainly younger than her own twenty-six, particularly the way she looked now. She was grateful for the dimness of the light. "You still working on that government review?" he asked.

She nodded. "If it isn't one thing, it's another. I'm being buried alive in paper work."

"I know," he said sympathetically. "Everything in triplicate or worse. Marge used to complain a lot about it."

"With good reason," Shelbie said feelingly, "believe me. Say, you wouldn't happen to know anyone who'd like to have a very prestigious position dumped in his or her lap, would you?"

"For example the presidency of the historical society? The way Marge dumped it in yours?" He shook his head. "Not at the moment. But why? Are you finally throwing in the towel? Going back into teaching?"

"In case you don't remember, I never picked up the towel in the first place, so I'm hardly throwing it in. If Elwood High had picked up my contract last year, I certainly wouldn't be doing *this,* which adds up to the same amount of work for roughly one-tenth the money. And if that job up at Argos works out for me, the society will definitely need a new president."

"Goodness, you don't sound very cheerful, Shelbie. Something wrong?"

She shook her head, and Dick's infectious smile spread to Shelbie's face. "Nothing new," she said. "Just this so-called review. You wouldn't believe some of the things they want to know in these forms."

His grin seemed to broaden into genuine amusement. "Yes, I would. I helped Lou fill out some forms like that a couple of years ago, some federal forms, than which there is nothing worse. Remember the 'war on crime' a few years ago?"

She nodded, her own smile turning a bit more genuine now. "I didn't realize it extended all the way out here in the boondocks. I thought that was for big cities and high crime areas."

He shrugged. "Maybe that is where all the good stuff went. What we got was a rug for our radio room. A government specification rug, at that. Proper pile thickness and depth, governmental colors, the whole bit. The only trouble was, the guy who runs the radio couldn't get his chair to roll on it, so we had to buy a mat—at our own expense—to put on the rug under his chair."

Shelbie laughed. "And I suppose your covered-up government specification rug cut down substantially on the local crime rate?"

Another shrug and a slight smile. "We haven't analyzed all the statistics yet, but—" He stopped, his eyes darting toward a point over her shoulder. "Did you hear something?"

"Me? No." She glanced backward nervously. "Did you?"

"I'm not sure, but . . . Where are the light switches?"

"Right here," she said, reaching out and flipping up the two switches next to the door. A half dozen fluorescent tubes in both rooms flickered into life.

Dick glanced around hurriedly, then walked silently across the room, past the ancient horse-drawn mowing machine, around the single-bladed plow and planter, to the swinging doors that led to the rest of the building.

"Locked?" he asked, and then, before she could answer, pushed at them lightly.

The doors swung back a few inches, then swung shut again. Beyond them were steps leading up to a broad hallway. The Senior Citizens Center was the first door on the left, she knew, and on the right was a large meeting room where once had been the school's assembly hall.

He pushed the doors open again, stepping partway through and looking around. He was silent, listening, and Shelbie shivered involuntarily.

"I think," she said, "that you are simply trying to scare me. First you prowl around outside making inexplicable noises, and now you're making believe there's something inside here besides the two of us."

He was silent another few seconds, then stepped back, letting the doors swing shut with a click.

"You're probably right," he said. "When you're on the night shift very long, you start hearing things every time you go past a dark corner. To tell the truth, I'll be glad to get back on days next week and let Vern wander around after dark. There are times I think he actually likes it."

Vern Hadley was another of the deputies—on vacation this week, if Shelbie remembered correctly.

"What are *you* doing out here, by the way?" Shelbie asked as they started back toward the door to the alley.

"Just patrolling," he said. "I come by here every couple of hours, especially since your maybe-break-in last week, and I just happened to see your light. Incidentally, did anyone ever remember—or confess to—leaving your door unlocked? Or are we still looking for a possible prowler?"

"No one's remembered, not for sure," Shelbie said, "but that must be what happened. Nobody found anything missing anywhere in the building. Not that there'd be much to take unless you're an antique freak."

Dick glanced around once more at the room full of farm equipment in various states of repair and disrepair. "Did you ever check to see if somebody left you something extra? Something they didn't want to bother taking all the way to the city dump . . . ?"

When Shelbie didn't answer, he took a last look into the inner room of the museum, then came back to stand by the outer door. "You're through for the night, you said?"

"Very much through." She flipped off the lights and pushed the door open. As Dick followed her into the alley, she located her keys, held them up at eye level for Dick to see, then inserted one into the lock, turned it until there was a loud click, and withdrew it.

"Locked," she said. "No forgetting this time." She dropped the keys into her purse and started across the alley toward the parking lot. Behind her, she heard a rattling. She turned. Dick was just releasing his hold on the door handle, apparently satisfied that, this time, the door really was locked.

The only trouble, Shelbie thought with a slight shiver as Dick waved his flashlight at her casually and started toward the Sheriff's Department car parked a dozen yards down the alley, was that she was ninety-nine percent sure she could remember doing exactly the same thing when she had left last Tuesday, the evening before the door had been found unlocked in the morning . . .

Suppressing another shiver that brushed at her spine, Shelbie turned and hurried toward the parking lot and the elderly Toyota that sat alone, waiting in the dim light from the single street lamp at the corner a hundred feet away.

Finally, there came a sound other than the voice that still pounded at her relentlessly. Something from the world outside her mind penetrated the shell she had erected around herself. A bird, somewhere in the trees that lined the lake a dozen yards beyond her window. A bird, which meant that dawn must finally, truly be coming.

She opened her eyes, and the silent scream that she had been holding tightly within herself during all the hours of darkness erupted like a coiled spring that had suddenly been released. It filled the room and battered at her ears and tore at her throat. And then it was gone. There was only the voice, still repeating its endless litany.

There was only the voice—and the sun, already shimmering its way through the leaves of the trees beyond her window, already at least a half hour above the horizon of the far shore of the lake.

The voice.

And the sun.

No longer was her madness confined to the night. No longer did the coming of dawn bring silence and peace. No longer . . .

Slowly, deliberately, she sat up, slid her feet out onto the threadbare carpet, and stood up. Her hand reached out to the bedside table and grasped the bottle of pills, still more than half full. With a final, aching look at the brightening world outside her window, she clutched the bottle tightly and moved across the floor toward the bathroom, her padding footsteps keeping macabre time with the voice that still pounded within her head.

CHAPTER 2

Shelbie came awake slowly, wondering whether the voice on the clock radio next to the bed belonged to Dolly Parton or Tammy Wynette. If only, she thought blearily, country-western types would stick to singing and not break into syrupy recitation at the slightest provocation.

Automatically, she stretched her arm across to the other side of the bed. C.G.? Had he already—

Then, abruptly, the half-dreaming euphoria vanished, and the memory of the last year and a half crowded back into her mind. For a moment, she wanted to retreat into the dreams of those earlier times long before the divorce, no matter how distorted she knew the dreams were. But it was only for a moment —a single, uncomfortable moment—and then she was throwing back the covers with more energy than was strictly necessary and climbing quickly to her feet. If C.G. were around, she thought as she wiggled her feet into the slippers next to the bed, the clock radio would have been hooked up to the stereo so they could be awakened by something he approved of, something classical. Not that there was anything wrong with Rossini or Wagner now and then, but they weren't what she wanted to wake up to. But, then, she thought ruefully, neither was that abominable interlude of recitation. It hadn't lasted long, luckily, and Whoever-It-Was was back to straight singing.

From the sunlight that streamed in through the bedroom window, it looked like it was going to be a good day, one that would be just right for hauling rocks. Now if only Harry Zartmann and his pickup truck came through as promised, she thought as she pulled a well-worn pair of jeans and an old blouse from the closet and tossed them on the bed. If Harry didn't show, she would have to either go scrounging for another truck or talk the guy at the gravel pit into hanging onto the rocks "for just another day or two," which was what she had been doing for the past three weeks already.

Finishing a quick breakfast, Shelbie hurried down the steps from the apartment, climbed into the Toyota parked at the end of the gravel drive that ran along the side of the house, got it started on the first try, and pulled out onto Madison. She detoured a few blocks to drive past the log cabin the historical society was building at the edge of the city park. Joe and Milt, the two retired construction workers who had been donating their time throughout the summer, were already there, measuring and marking something along one of the incompleted walls. They looked up and waved as she drove by.

Shelbie had just pulled into the museum parking lot when Harry showed up with his elderly but heavily sprung truck. She paused only long enough to take a quick look inside the museum to be sure Cindy Marsh was indeed there, her typewriter clattering away at the stacks of fund and membership solicitation letters. Reassured, she hurried to Harry's truck and climbed in.

Two hours later, they were back. The truck's springs, heavy as they were, were barely holding up under the load, a dozen almost-flat rocks from a gravel pit a few miles southeast of town, and Shelbie was not looking forward to helping Harry with the unloading.

The problem solved itself, though, when Tim Remington, Marge Remington's sixteen-year-old came within hailing distance.

"Tim! Got a minute?" Shelbie flagged him down as he went past the alley, heading downtown at his usual long-legged, gangling pace.

He stopped and looked around, recognizing the voice. He hesitated a moment. Then: "I guess I do. Why?"

"We've got a load of flat rocks from the gravel pit. We're

going to use them for historical markers—if we can get them out of the truck and into the museum, that is."

Tim's eyes widened. "Those things weigh a *ton!*" he said, probably remembering the boulders that his mother, who had been president before Shelbie, had erected here and there around the county.

"These aren't quite that big," Shelbie reassured him as he approached, "although I wouldn't mind getting a few like that. No, these are only a couple hundred pounds."

"Oh. These are just for insignificant historical sites?"

Shelbie laughed. "Something like that. Now do you feel like giving us a hand, or—"

"Okay," he said, glancing at the truck. "But I can't stick around very long. Gotta get my column in pretty soon." He tapped a folded sheet of paper stuck in his shirt pocket.

Shelbie raised an eyebrow. "Old C.G. is getting generous? Didn't you just have one in the *Sentinel* a couple of days ago?"

"Yeah, but this is something special, a review of that crummy monster movie that's opening at the drive-in tonight. Another evil-possession cheapie. That's all they're making these days, ever since *The Exorcist*. And believe me, this is no *Exorcist.*"

"It starts tonight? And you've already seen it? Or are you just exercising your youthful prerogative to prejudge?"

The boy shook his head loosely if indignantly. "I saw it down at Logan last night. I talked Mom into letting me have the car, since this was sort of an official newspaper assignment."

"Sure it was, Tim. Is C.G. paying you enough for the review to cover the cost of the gas? Or even the ticket?"

Tim shrugged. "You gotta start somewhere. And he's paying more than you're probably going to for moving these rocks. Incidentally, where do they go?"

"Over in the corner by the box wagon for now," she said, and then hurried to hold the door open as Tim and Harry struggled to get the first rock out of the truck and into the museum. As they disappeared into the interior, Shelbie peered around the floor near the door, located the wooden doorstop, and wedged it firmly in place.

A second later, Cindy Marsh came trotting out between the wagons and rakes. She was a small, squarish-faced girl in her early twenties, even shorter than Shelbie, and probably twenty pounds lighter despite the seemingly endless parade of Cokes and Twinkies and pizzas she consumed the way other people smoked cigarettes. Cindy was one of the girls being paid through CETA, which was one of the U.S. government's red-tape employment programs. She was also one of the girls whose jobs were being reviewed by whoever it was in Washington that did that sort of thing. The only one currently working, as a matter of fact. One had left a month ago, and another was taking a week off, but Shelbie still had to fill out forms on all three. Trying to fill them out "meaningfully" was, of course, an exercise in futility, and at the moment, Shelbie couldn't even remember precisely which office the reviewer "worked out of."

"You remember that pewter lump, the one in the odds-and-ends case?" Cindy asked when she was within a few yards of Shelbie. Cindy was not one to waste time on irrelevancies like "hello."

"Pewter?" For an instant, Shelbie's mind was a blank, but then, remembering, she blinked. It was the same figure that had caught her eye briefly last night. And in a way, Cindy was right. It was something of a lump, something whose identity they weren't sure of. The only suggestion anyone had ever made after looking at the ugly Easter Island face, was that it was a piece out of a two-hundred-year-old chess set—maybe a knight, since knights tended normally to be a little weirder-looking than the other pieces. The only reason they knew it was pewter was that a collector who had come through last spring had identified it.

"I've never seen anything like it," the woman had said, "especially that old. And you can tell by the surface that it's old, very old. Why, I wouldn't be surprised if— But I do wonder who made it. Most pewterers that long ago made mostly conventional, useful items—plates, trays, mugs, that sort of thing. But this . . ."

"I know the one you mean," Shelbie said to Cindy. "I was just looking at it last night, as a matter of fact."

"Oh? Well, someone else was looking at it this morning."

"And he told you what it really was?"

"Hardly. I don't think he even knew it was pewter. Anyway, he asked what it was, and when I told him it was a pewter mystery lump, he wanted to know where we got it."

"So you told him, and that was that?"

Cindy shook her head. "No, and that's where the mystery really comes in. I couldn't find it listed in any of our files. I sort of hoped you might know something about it."

"Not if it's not in our faultless file system," Shelbie said. "You're positive it's not listed? What's the acquisition number?"

"Aha!" Cindy said with a show of mock triumph. "Now you begin to grasp the problem. There is no acquisition number. And I couldn't find anything in the alphabetical listings, either."

"No number? Let's take another look, Cindy," Shelbie said, leading the way back to the main room.

But there was nothing. The number normally inked onto an obscure portion of an exhibit and then shellacked over was missing. Nor was there an identifying tag attached to it, as there was to some of the older exhibits. And there was no alphabetical card under any of the headings either of them could think of—pewter, chess, knight, pawn, bust, figure, demon, Easter Island, even lump.

"Must've been brought in before they started putting the number directly on the item," Cindy commented. "But still it should have a tag."

"True, unless it got lost, which is a possibility. Some of these things were stored in all sorts of strange places before we—or Marge Remington, actually—promoted all this display space."

Cindy shrugged. "Maybe it was left anonymously on our

doorstep one dark and rainy night, like that horrendous owl must've been." She squinted at the tiny demonic face.

Shelbie held the pewter figure close, studying the workmanship more than the features. Like all pewter, it was cast, and, from this close, it looked more than a little crude—almost amateurish. The features were irregular, a bit lopsided, and it certainly didn't look completely human. Not even caricature human, but just plain alien. As Shelbie had thought before, a hollow-cheeked, sinister-looking miniature version of the Easter Island monoliths.

She shook her head, handing the figure back to Cindy. "Here, put it back in the case. I'd better get back out there to supervise the rocks."

"No other ideas?" Cindy asked, taking the figure in her hand.

"Not unless you want to go through our donor file, one card at a time, looking for something that might fit the description."

"No, thanks. But what about Marge? Maybe she'd remember something?"

"It's possible," Shelbie said. "Who asked about it, anyway?"

"A man, but he didn't say who he was. Said he'd be back, though, when I told him you'd be in later this morning and you might know something about it."

"Didn't he sign the guest book?"

Cindy shook her head. "He said he'd be back, so . . ."

"Did he at least say why he was interested?"

"Just that he was curious. He thought the face looked 'unusual.' "

"That's one way of putting it." Shelbie frowned thoughtfully. "You don't suppose he recognized it, do you?"

"That thing? Hardly. Not unless he's been to one of Tim's monster movies."

"*The Teeny Tiny Horror in the Museum,*" Shelbie said, laughing despite—or perhaps because of—the memory of the night before. "Now, I don't want to change the subject too abruptly, but have you come up with a good guess as to how many letters you've typed since you've been here?"

"A guess, but I don't know how good it is. I mean, after all, I didn't know the government was going to audit me. Anyway, the guess is on your desk, more or less on top. And I called Mrs. Cole—you know, about all that research we did for her club. She's got copies of everything we sent her, and she said she'd be glad to write a testimonial for us, or anything else we want."

"I doubt that we'll need anything that elaborate right now, but one of these days it might come in handy. It might be a good idea for her to write up something now, just so we can have it on file in case some 'inspector' descends on us unexpectedly. How long were you and Alice on that project, anyway?"

"Off and on for a couple of weeks, at least. And if anyone doesn't believe we could take that long to do some simple ancestor research for a small club full of old women, just send him to me. I'll be happy to take him on a tour of all those old records and junk we dug through, unreadable handwriting, misspellings, and all."

Shelbie grinned. "I doubt that it will come to that, but I'll remember you made the offer. Just you remember, though, if anyone like that does come around, checking up on those forms I'm sending in, he's the one who's paying your salary. Or at least he could have a loud voice in getting it cut off. And he might even be able to get that other program started up again so Velma could come back for another month or two."

"I know," Cindy admitted. "So I shouldn't tell him what I'm really thinking. Or what you're thinking either, right? I promise I'll be tactful."

Cindy, who had been leaning down to open the rear of the display case, stopped and straightened. Her eyes looked over Shelbie's shoulder, and her expression indicated that Shelbie should do the same.

An instant later, Shelbie became aware of the footsteps on the concrete floor behind her. For whatever reason—perhaps a reaction left over from the night before, perhaps a reaction to Cindy's sudden look—Shelbie felt a faint tingle play across her back, and she spun around quickly toward the approaching footsteps.

The man walking toward her, she realized immediately, looked familiar. He was a bit less than six feet tall, large, but not necessarily overweight. His face was broad and somewhat rounded despite a squarish look to his jaw. His hair, brown and almost straight, was short enough so that the lack of recent combing didn't make a lot of difference. His grey trousers didn't match the brown jacket, and the entire effect, including the open-collared white shirt, was of someone on the verge of looking rumpled.

After a second, a grin spread across his face as he looked at Shelbie, and she wondered momentarily if her jeans and dark blouse had sustained more damage or dirt from the rock hauling than she had thought.

"Shelbie Wilson, right?" he asked, and as he spoke, the name and all the rest came back. She laughed suddenly at the unexpectedness of it.

"Matt Decker," she said. "What are *you* doing back here? I thought you'd left long ago to make your fortune in the big city."

"If you call Claymore a big city, and if you call a so-so salary for technical writing making a fortune, you might be right." He looked for a second as if he were going to give her a quick hug, but after a brief hesitation, he clasped his hands around one of hers in an awkward movement that wasn't quite a handshake.

When he released her hand, Shelbie glanced toward Cindy, who was standing by, looking interested. Shelbie flushed slightly. "My first starry-eyed—well, puppy-love affair might describe it," she explained hurriedly. "He was a glamorous senior on the staff of the high school newspaper when I was a freshman. I always was—always used to be a sucker for writers of any kind," she finished in a rush, and then, before anyone else could say more along those lines, she asked, "You're the mysterious stranger who was asking about our pewter oddity?"

He blinked at the sudden change of subject. "Yes." A glance at Cindy, still standing a foot or so to Shelbie's left, in front of the owl at the end of the display case. "She said the boss might be able to tell me more about it."

Shelbie shook her head. "Sorry, but it doesn't look as if I can. We haven't been able to locate anything at all in our files. And there isn't even an acquisition number on it." She smiled faintly. "To tell the embarrassing truth, I'm not even sure what it is."

For an instant, his eyes seemed to narrow and his features harden, but it was so brief that Shelbie found herself wondering if it had happened at all.

"There's no other way of finding out where it came from?" he asked. "Or what it is?"

"Well," Shelbie said slowly, "there are a couple of possibilities, but they're both pretty remote."

Again the momentary flicker of his features, but again it was gone before it could completely register in Shelbie's mind.

"If it's a matter of money," he began, "I'm sure I could—"

"No, nothing like that," Shelbie said hastily. "Not that we can't use all the donations—and memberships—we can get, but that has nothing to do with it. The problem is that we can't find it in the alphabetical lists and, as I said before, there's no acquisition number on it, which means we can't look it up in the numerical file. The only chance would be for someone to go through all our files, card by card, looking for an entry for it. And there may not be—probably isn't—any such entry."

"Possibly I could go through the files myself?"

Shelbie shrugged. "You're welcome to try. We have several thousand items, though. And I suspect our paper work and records just haven't kept up with all our new display space. Most of these things were stored away for years, and considering the fact that the society has gone through a dozen presidents in the last twenty years, there isn't all that much continuity, I'm afraid."

He hesitated. "You said 'a couple of possibilities,' didn't you? Which means there's another way of attacking the problem?"

Shelbie nodded. "We could talk to Marge Remington. She

was president for a few years before I was—before I took it over. She might remember something, but the chances are slim."

"Remington . . ." He frowned thoughtfully. "I seem to remember that name. Wasn't she the one who tried to run some kind of recreation center about the time we were in school?"

Shelbie nodded again, laughing. "Among other enterprises, yes. For a while she was running a poker game in her basement, complete with house cuts. A slightly different kind of recreation center, I suppose. And now she's trying to make a go of a weekly newspaper, the *Bugle*."

"I remember her now," he said, chuckling. "In fact, I think my dad may've been one of her poker players once in a while. Wasn't she running the poker game at the same time she was running the recreation center?"

"I think they overlapped a little, but then, her projects usually did."

"You said she was head of the historical society?" His voice had a tinge of disbelief. "When was that?"

"Before the weekly paper and after the poker game. There may have been something else for a while in between, but I'm not sure. Somewhere along the line, I know, she worked as a nurse at one of the factories down in Logan."

He shook his head. "How did she ever get mixed up with the historical society? Does it pay well?"

"Hardly! But for Marge, it wasn't the money, it was the connections. You'd be surprised how many upstanding citizens you can meet through this job." Or how many you *have* to meet, Shelbie thought ruefully, depending on how you look at it. But Marge was always looking out for herself—that was for sure. In fact, it had been a couple of contacts made through the society—a mayor, a couple of businessmen, and a couple of "prominent" families—who had put up the money for her to start the *Bugle*. Those and one or two of the ex-poker players.

"Is she still in town?" Matt asked.

"Very much so," Shelbie said. "In fact, that's her son carting rocks out there in the other room. You must've seen him on your way in."

"Oh?" He turned halfway toward the door behind him, then looked back at Shelbie. "Then you wouldn't have any trouble contacting her? Asking her about the figure?"

Shelbie shook her head. "Probably not. Although you might have trouble catching her at home. I'm not sure what her schedule is, but I think she's about ready to put out another issue, and—"

Shelbie broke off as the phone rang, and Cindy darted over to Shelbie's desk and picked up the receiver. A moment later, she held it out toward Shelbie.

"It's someone at Denniston's office," Cindy said, looking questioningly at Shelbie.

Shelbie frowned puzzledly, then shrugged as she started toward the phone. "You check with Tim, why don't you, Cindy? See if Marge is going to be home today."

Cindy nodded as she handed the receiver to Shelbie and, smiling, walked slowly past Matt on her way to the outer room and Tim.

"Shelbie Wilson speaking. What can I do for you?"

"Probably nothing," the phone said, and Shelbie immediately recognized the voice of Kate Miller, Phil Denniston's secretary, "but I thought it was worth a call to find out, since you're more or less responsible for our hiring her."

Shelbie sighed. "Don't tell me Carla is giving you a problem." Carla Schaeffer had worked for the museum for several months on CETA funding, the same as Cindy, but then Shelbie had heard about the opening for a file clerk in Denniston's office. And, since CETA was supposed to be strictly temporary, a sort of "training ground," it was only logical that Carla should take another job when one appeared. She had been doing fairly well, Shelbie thought, at least until the last week or so.

"More or less of a problem," Kate was saying. "We haven't been able to locate Carla at all today."

"She didn't come to work?"

"No, she didn't, and not so much as a word from her, either. I even tried calling her at home, but there was no answer." Kate was the model of an efficient worker, and she had trouble even imagining the workings of the mind of someone who wasn't. "You haven't heard from her?"

"Not for a few days," Shelbie said hesitantly.

"Did she say anything then to indicate she might be quitting?"

"Not really, but . . . Did you let the phone ring very long?"

"A half dozen times. That's surely enough. After all, her house isn't all that large."

"Normally, it would be enough, but Carla was having trouble sleeping last week. I think she was planning to get something to help her if it didn't clear up."

"You think she could still be sleeping? At this time of day?" The idea of someone sleeping under any circumstances after 10 A.M. was obviously beyond Kate's comprehension.

"Stranger things have been known to happen, Kate. Would you like me to try calling her myself?"

"If you wish. But do you know of anywhere else she might be? Anyone she might be—staying with?" The disapproving tone was plain in Kate's voice.

"No one that I know of. I'll let you know if I get in touch with her." Shelbie hung up, cutting Kate's obligatory "Thank you" in half. She glanced toward the door, saw that both Cindy and Matt were still in the next room, then flipped open the card file of addresses next to the phone. It took only a few seconds to locate and dial Carla's number.

On the fifteenth ring, Cindy and Matt walked back into the room. Cindy looked at Shelbie questioningly.

"Trying to call Carla," Shelbie explained, then waited for another two rings and hung up. Frowning, she looked at the file card again and redialed. This time she gave up after eight rings. Where could Carla have gone? She wasn't the type to just—

"What's going on?" Cindy asked.

Shelbie shook her head. "Carla didn't show up at the office

today, and now I can't raise her at home. But what did you find out about Marge?"

"According to Tim, she should be home at least until noon. Tim says this is the morning she does her gossip column for the paper."

Shelbie glanced at her watch, then at Matt. "You shouldn't have any trouble, then, if you want to see her today."

"No, but . . . Would it be possible for me to take the figure along? To show her what I'm talking about?" He looked toward the figure in the display case. "It might help her to remember it."

"I'm sorry, but . . ." The thought of Carla intruded on Shelbie's thoughts. After a second, she looked up at Matt again. "If you could wait a little while, say an hour or so, I could check with her myself. But I want to— You heard what we were talking about?"

"Someone's missing from work? Yes, I heard."

"Carla used to work here, and in a way I feel responsible for her—for her job at Denniston's, anyway. And she did sound upset when she talked to me last week." She glanced at Cindy. "I think I'll drive out to her cottage and take a look, just to be on the safe side. I can take the figure with me and stop at Marge's on the way back. Would that be all right, Matt?"

"Certainly. I'm in no great rush, but . . . Look, why don't I go along with you? I don't have any other pressing business."

Cindy grinned briefly but cut it short as Shelbie glanced toward her. Cindy hurriedly opened the display case and handed the figure to Shelbie. "You want me to call Marge and tell her you'll be stopping by in a little while?" the girl asked.

Shelbie hesitated. "All right," she said finally, "tell her it'll be a half hour, maybe forty-five minutes."

"You never did tell me what brought you back to Elwood, Matt," Shelbie said as she pulled out onto Main Street.

Matt, his substantial, not-quite-six-feet fitted into the passenger's side of her Toyota, looked toward her. He seemed to be thinking, considering.

"Just trying to get my uncle's estate settled," he said.

"Uncle?"

"Ben Cunningham. My mother's brother."

"Cunningham?" The name clicked into place immediately, and she darted a look toward him. "I didn't know—Cunningham of the mansion was your uncle?"

He chuckled and made a deprecatory gesture with his hands. "He owned a pretty big place out on the lake, yes."

"I'll be—" She shook her head. "If I'd known that back in high school . . . You realize, I hope, that never getting inside that house to explore—that house and a dozen others—has been one of my lifelong frustrations?"

Another chuckle, though his expression was a bit rueful. "I doubt that I could've done you much good. I was never inside the place myself either—at least not after I was five or six years old."

"Oh? Don't tell me—" She stopped abruptly as, belatedly, she remembered the nature of Ben Cunningham's death. She glanced toward Matt a second later as they rolled to a stop at a red light. He was looking at her, and she snatched her eyes back to the street.

"No need to be embarrassed," he said as the light changed and she depressed the accelerator and made the turn to the east, out of Elwood toward the lake. "He committed suicide. There's no secret about it."

"I'm sorry." Automatic words, she thought, as meaningless as most apologies.

"I'm not sure I am," he said a moment later. "Sorry, that is." He went on as she glanced toward him, her eyebrows raised. "I hadn't seen him for nearly twenty-five years. I told you I hadn't seen the inside of the house since I was five or so. And I never did know him at all well, so I certainly can't be very grief-stricken about his death. And since my mother and I seem to be the sole surviving relatives . . ." He shrugged and leaned back in the seat.

"You're honest, at least," Shelbie said.

"At least. And why not?" A trace of bitterness entered his

voice. "He was certainly well enough off, and he never did a thing for my mother while he was alive."

"Family feud?"

He shrugged again. "Maybe. Pretty one-sided, for all I could tell."

"He was the one doing the feuding?"

Another shrug. "That's the way it seemed. Although I never did hear his side of the story, so I suppose anything's possible."

"You don't sound convinced."

"After hearing one side of the story for twenty-odd years, one tends to become a bit prejudiced," he said. "According to my mother, he simply 'severed relations' with us, as they say in the diplomatic corps. One day he was friendly old Uncle Ben, the next day he moved into that house, and then . . ." Matt lapsed into silence as they neared the edge of town. "That was almost twenty-five years ago," he went on, bitterness again evident in his voice, "and to all intents and purposes, that's the last any of us ever saw of him except for one visit, which we'd have been better off not making. From then on, he was either shut up in that house or off traveling somewhere. Or so we used to read in the papers."

He settled back into silence again, and this time Shelbie, after a brief glance at his solemn features, followed suit for the few minutes it took to reach the lake.

The house—cottage, really—where Carla had lived since her father died the year before, was three or four miles from town, on the western shore of the lake. The road that cut over from the highway was a narrow, winding blacktop that paralleled the lake shore fifty or a hundred yards away.

Carla's four-room, year-round house was one of a dozen or so that shared a dusty, dead-end road—or communal driveway —that curved away from the main road a hundred yards beyond the edge of a golf course on the opposite side of the road. Carla's was the last in line. Beyond it to the south, after a hundred yards of gradually lengthening grass, the woods themselves began. In some places it was more swamp than woods, particularly around the Mound—an Indian burial mound, according to the least spectacular of the local legends—but after another half mile, the ground solidified again and a second string of cottages began.

The front porch of Carla's house was a single concrete step, but the back porch, facing the lake, was screened and it covered most of the back of the building. Along the north side of the narrow lot, next to the hedge that shielded it from the next cottage, was a gravel drive.

In the drive, facing in toward the lake, was Carla's red and slightly rusty subcompact station wagon.

Gravel crunched under the Toyota's wheels as it rolled to a stop behind the other car. As Shelbie shut off the engine, the distant sound of a motorboat drifted in from the lake.

"Her car?" Matt asked.

Shelbie nodded but made no immediate move to get out of the car. Her eyes were on the cottage, watching nothing, seeing only the random pattern the scattered sunbeams made as they erratically pierced the trees that stood over the house. Any second now, she told herself, Carla will notice my car and stick her head out the door and yell at me.

But she wouldn't, and somehow Shelbie knew it.

Reluctantly, feeling much the way she had the night before in the darkened museum, Shelbie climbed out. Last night it had been the darkness that had seemed to be hiding something. Now it was the walls of the cottage.

"Want me to come with you?" Matt was standing next to the car, watching her.

She shook her head. "No, I'll be just a second," she said, and, using the words as a springboard, she hurried across the grass to the front door.

She pressed the bell, and then, when she couldn't hear any corresponding sound from inside, knocked firmly. Again she knocked, but still there was no response. Carla could, Shelbie supposed, be sleeping *really* deeply . . .

Following the narrow concrete walkway around the side of the house, Shelbie went to the screened-in porch at the back and knocked again. As she stood waiting, she glanced toward the car. Matt was still standing next to it, looking at her questioningly.

Finally, after several more seconds of knocking and waiting, Shelbie turned away from the door, toward the window just beyond the porch. The window was closed, but there were no drapes, and the curtains were filmy, almost transparent. Carla's bedroom, she remembered from the one time she had been inside.

With an odd combination of reluctance and urgency, Shelbie moved toward the window and leaned close, shading her eyes against the glare of the sun. A moment later, as her eyes adjusted to the relative dimness of the interior, the faint apprehension that had been hovering inside her suddenly exploded, sending a shock wave through her entire body, forcing a moan from her lips.

Stretched out on top of the rumpled bed, barely a yard from the window, one arm dangling limply over the edge, the fingers almost touching the threadbare carpet, was Carla.

CHAPTER 3

"Is something wrong?"

Matt's voice seemed to come from a great distance, as if he were part of another world. Shelbie glanced in his direction and saw him hurrying toward her. The momentary paralysis left her.

"It's Carla!" she said at the same instant she started toward the door to the porch. It was unhooked, as it usually was, but the inner door, leading to the kitchen, was locked. Shelbie was rattling the knob and pushing at it futilely when Matt came to a stop next to her.

"I saw through the window," he said shortly. "What happened?"

"How should I know? She was having trouble sleeping, so—" She broke off, looking hurriedly around the enclosed porch. "We've got to get in there!" she said, then spotted an empty flowerpot in one corner.

Before she could reach the pot, Matt snatched it up, and, standing to one side, smashed it into the corner of the door window, sending glass showering to the floor both inside and out. Pushing the loose splinters of glass from the frame, he reached through and unlocked the door. Shelbie darted through ahead of him, through the kitchen and into the bedroom.

"Carla!" The instant Shelbie touched the girl's face, she knew they were too late. There was a pallor, a coldness that seemed to chill the entire room despite the sun that still streamed in through the window.

Shelbie pulled her hand back sharply and stood up. An instant later, she felt strong hands grasping her shoulders, holding her steady, and it was only then that she realized she had been backing blindly away from the sprawled form on the bed.

Shelbie waited outside while Matt phoned the sheriff. She was standing at the water's edge when he came out a few minutes later, his face grim.

"Someone'll be along in a few minutes," he said, then stood silently behind her, looking out across the water. The power boat they had heard before was in the middle of the lake, and two others skimmed along the far shore, perhaps a mile away, towing a pair of water skiers.

"On purpose, you think?" His quiet words jolted Shelbie out of the shell she had been trying—unsuccessfully—to erect around herself.

"Carla? Of course not! What would ever give you an idea like that?" Her defense of Carla was automatic, as it would be of anyone who was as young as she had been—younger than Shelbie herself.

"You mentioned she had been having trouble sleeping recently," he said, still quietly.

"A little insomnia is hardly a reason for suicide!"

"I know. But there was a prescription bottle of some kind— the only word I could make out without picking it up was 'sleep.' The bottle was in the bathroom, empty."

"What?" Shelbie spun around to face him, not sure where the sudden surge of anger had come from. "What were you doing in there? You didn't even know her, and you—"

"I'm sorry," he said, and this time the words sounded as if they meant something—not the way they had sounded when Shelbie herself had said them a few minutes earlier. "I know I shouldn't have, but . . . Just say it's a morbid curiosity, brought on by my uncle's doing himself in."

As quickly as it had come, the anger was gone, and Shelbie found herself apologizing to him. In his place, she knew, she probably would have done the same thing. It was only the fact that Carla had been a friend, the fact that Shelbie had been partly overcome by shock, that had kept her from searching through the house herself. If it had been a stranger in there . . .

The best way to survive those next few hours or days, she realized, was to be as objective as possible about everything, to do her best to divorce herself from whatever feelings she had had about Carla. To think of her and her actions logically, as if she *had* been a stranger.

And thinking logically meant that, no matter what Shelbie might feel emotionally, Carla was just as likely to have committed suicide as anyone else. "She wasn't the type" was what the friends or relatives of suicides almost invariably said. No one ever appeared to be the type—until after the body was found.

"I understand," she said finally. "At least I think I do. If I hadn't been so shaken up, I probably would've been searching the place myself." She looked up at him. *"Do* you think it was intentional?"

He shook his head, glancing toward the road for a moment. "I don't know. You'd be in a better position to guess than I would. You talked to her recently, you said. I didn't even know her."

Shelbie forced a faint smile. "It doesn't look as if I knew her very well either. I certainly didn't expect anything like this."

"No one ever does," Matt said, echoing Shelbie's own thoughts of moments before. "Like my uncle. Plenty of money, not a worry in the world that anyone knew of, but still he did it. Or at least that was the verdict at the inquest."

Briefly, the sinking feeling, the slight twinge of nausea that she had felt inside the cottage, reasserted itself, and she purposely took a deep breath and looked away from the cottage, out across the lake. She realized she was having trouble coping with the simple fact of Carla's death, let alone the possibility—probability—that it was suicide.

"I suppose there will have to be an inquest," she said quietly, her voice tenser than she had intended.

"Whenever there's any doubt whatsoever about the cause of

death," Matt said. "Or so they said when I asked them about my uncle."

"Did—did they ever find out why he did it?" By focusing her attention on another death—the death of a stranger—perhaps she could keep her thoughts away from Carla.

"Not a clue. More or less perfect health, except for a mild touch of arthritis, according to his doctor, which certainly isn't unusual for a man in his fifties. Certainly no money problems that anyone knew about. And, since he was never married, no marital problems." He shrugged, then looked down at her. "What about your friend? Any problems that you knew of?"

Shelbie shook her head, more vigorously than necessary. "Her father died a couple of years ago, but she seemed to have gotten over that pretty well. And she didn't have any money troubles that I know of. She inherited this cottage from her father, and her job at Denniston's office paid reasonably well. For around here, at least."

"Boyfriends?"

"No one special. Not that I knew about, anyway. But, then, we weren't really all that close. There could've been someone easily enough." She managed to keep her voice steady despite the trembling she felt in her throat. "I knew her mostly because she used to work in the museum, before she went to Denniston's."

He paused, looking down at her, apparently sensing the tension that was still in her. "Would you rather not talk about it now?"

Shelbie forced another unsteady smile. "Frankly, I don't know right this minute what I want. But maybe I'd better see if I can get rid of these shakes before anyone official starts asking the same questions."

"Whatever you want. No talk at all while you collect your thoughts? Want to talk about the museum? What you've been doing since high school?"

"All of burning interest, I'm sure." Her voice was steady again. "No, I'd better stick to the subject at hand. And I think I'll be all right as long as I don't have to go back inside." She shivered as she glanced back at the cottage. "I'm just glad it's broad daylight on a sunny day."

For the next five minutes, they stuck to the subject. As Shelbie had hoped, the words came more easily and more steadily each minute, and by the time Lou Rokane, the sheriff, arrived, she was almost fully in control again. Neither she nor Matt, however, were any the wiser about possible reasons Carla might have had to commit suicide.

When Shelbie told Rokane about the sleeping pills, he swore under his breath and shook his head. "It's getting to be an epidemic!" he said after a moment, still frowning and shaking his head. "Do you know how many that makes? Just in the last—" He broke off, looking sharply at Matt. "What did you say your name was?"

"Matthew Decker. My uncle—"

The sheriff snapped his fingers as he apparently made the connection. "Ben Cunningham! I should've remembered right off. He's the one that set off this rash!"

When Shelbie and Matt both looked at him puzzledly, he went on. "I'm not saying he had anything to do with any of this, but—he *was* the first!"

"First what? Suicide?" Matt's brow creased in a thoughtful frown, and Shelbie found herself listening uneasily. She was just getting over finding Carla's body, and now— "How many have there been?" Matt asked quietly.

Sheriff Rokane snorted. "She's number five," he said, inclining his head toward the cottage. "All in three months! We don't usually have that many in three *years!*"

The subject obviously disturbed Rokane personally, not just as a sheriff. Something seemed to be prodding him, keeping him talking. It was as if he had been saving it up since the first, since Matt's uncle had "started" the epidemic. "And you know what's really insane?" he went on. "Except for your uncle, they've all been practically kids, like Miss Schaeffer in there. Not a one out of their twenties, if you can believe it!"

Abruptly, it dawned on Shelbie why Rokane was talking the way he was, why he was so upset. His own daughter, Joan, an only child, was about that age. Shelbie remembered her in one of the first English classes she had taught in Elwood. Joan had been a junior then, and that had been five years ago.

"Were they all the same?' Matt was asking. "Sleeping pills every one?" Despite her sudden understanding and sympathy for Rokane, Shelbie listened intently for an answer.

"Every one!" Rokane said, again shaking his head sharply. "I just hope this one finally ends it!"

"No connections between any of them?" Matt asked. "Nothing at all?"

"Connections?" The sheriff looked at him blankly. "You mean were any of them friends? Or relatives?"

Matt blinked, as if for a moment he weren't sure himself just what he had meant. "Something like that," he said finally. "Any kind of connection at all. Same high school class. All left-handed. Anything."

Sheriff Rokane frowned, suspicion clouding his face. "Not that anyone has noticed," he said. "But then, nobody's looked all that hard before. Are you driving at something?"

Matt shook his head. "Just curious, that's all. After all, as you said, my uncle started this whole thing, and I would like to know . . ." His voice trailed off, and his face became thoughtful. "There isn't any doubt that they were all suicides, is there?"

"When someone takes a bottleful of sleeping pills, there's not much room for doubt," the sheriff said flatly.

"Did any of them leave notes? My uncle didn't."

Rokane's frown deepened. "Look, Decker, if you have any ideas about this, let's have them!"

"No, nothing," Matt said hastily, and Shelbie couldn't help noticing a faintly puzzled look on his face as he spoke.

The sheriff continued to frown at Matt, his eyes narrowing. "I'm telling you, Decker," he said, underlining his words with short, choppy gestures of his right hand, "if you know something about these suicides, you let me know!" The voice was quiet, menacing, and just a little afraid. Though the fear was not, Shelbie was sure, for himself. "If you do know something, and you're keeping quiet about it, except to make these cryptic little remarks, I'm warning you—if there's another of these deaths, you're the first person I'll be looking for!"

When Matt said nothing, Rokane turned sharply toward Shelbie, his face now set in a scowl. His eyes met hers for an instant, and Shelbie could see the worry hidden beneath the granitelike features. If there were another death that followed the same pattern as the last four, it could well be his own daughter. . . .

Abruptly, he turned from them both and strode back to the cottage.

Matt let his breath out in a faint sigh, and some of the tension seemed to ease out of him. Shelbie looked at him puzzledly.

"Matt, *is* there something that—"

He shook his head sharply. "Nothing. Nothing at all. It's just— No, nothing." He glanced toward the sheriff, standing outside the back door, his eyes narrow as he watched them.

"Come on," Matt said. "We were on our way to see Mrs. Remington, weren't we? Are we still going?"

"Marge?" Shelbie blinked, disoriented for a moment, but then she remembered. Her hand went to her purse, where the pewter figure still lay, wrapped in layers of tissue to protect it from the rest of the debris she carried. It seemed as if ages had passed since she had put it there.

"Yes," she said slowly, "I suppose we may as well."

Carefully keeping her eyes averted from the bedroom window of the cottage, Shelbie walked back to the car. Matt followed and climbed in without a word. As she backed out and pulled away down the dusty road, she recognized the coroner's massive station wagon as it pulled off the main road and passed her, heading for the cottage.

Marge Remington, somewhere in her forties, was more or less a redhead this week, although the hair tended toward orange here and there. The last time Shelbie had seen her, about a month earlier, she had been more or less a blonde. Once, when she had been running the historical society, she had even been a brunette for a few months. As always, she was wearing a brightly colored pant suit—one that almost matched her hair this time—that looked slightly rumpled. A grey-and-white cat with a tail that looked like one of Orson Bean's paper eucalyptus trees shambled out through the kitchen door as Marge opened it for Shelbie and Matt.

"Don't mind Huntzie," she said, waving a hand in the direction of the disappearing cat. "He's the original 'grass is greener over the fence' kid. Whenever the door opens, he goes through, no matter whether he's in or out." She laughed raucously. "Like a lot of people I know. Maybe even a little like myself. Which reminds me—either of you interested in buying out a more-or-less-thriving weekly newspaper? No? I didn't really think so, but if you hear of anyone who is interested, let me know. Okay?"

"As long as it's not a friend," Shelbie said, grinning in spite of a momentary twinge of guilt at the way she seemed to be recovering so quickly from Carla's death now that she was out of sight of the cottage.

"And who's this?" Marge eyed an uncomfortable-looking Matt appreciatively.

Sighing, Shelbie introduced him.

"Well, it's about time," Marge said, a couple of seconds before the introduction was completed. "That other turkey's been out of your life for how long? Two years?"

"Almost. But if you don't knock off the hints pretty soon, I'll start throwing spare men at *you*."

"Sorry," Marge said, but she didn't look as if she regretted a thing. She looked Matt over again, her eyes roaming from face to feet and back up. "But if you ever do start throwing away your spares, you can start with this one. . . ."

"Be my guest," Shelbie said, making a slight bow as she glanced toward Matt, who was still looking slightly awkward at being the subject of the conversation. "But before you start your frontal attack, we've got a question for you. Something relatively official."

Marge sighed. "I knew it couldn't be that easy. Sure, come

on in." She stood back from the door, waving them through like someone introducing a tap-dance act to an invisible audience in the kitchen. "Now, what can I do for you?" she asked once they were seated around the dining-room table, which was covered with a portable typewriter and innumerable sheets of loose paper, most of which were covered with Marge's illegible note-taking scrawl.

"We were wondering about this," Shelbie said, taking the pewter figure from her purse and removing the tissue from around it. "It was in one of the display cases at the museum, but I couldn't find any information at all. No acquisition number, no card in the alphabetical files, nothing."

"And you hoped that I'd be able to remember it, right?" Marge held out her hand and took the figure. "Ugly little devil, isn't it?" she said, holding it close to her face and grimacing. "What is it?"

"That's what we were hoping you would be able to tell us," Shelbie said. "You don't remember it, then?"

Marge pursed her lips as she continued to look at the figure closely. "I'm not sure. It looks familiar, but . . . That is, I know I've seen it before, but I can't for the life of me remember where or when."

"I wasn't really expecting anything," Shelbie admitted. "Thanks anyway."

"Hold on, don't give up so fast. Give me a minute to think. Like I said, I definitely remember seeing it somewhere." Marge continued to stare at the object, turning it over thoughtfully in her hands. "Something that's been around a long time, I think. Probably from somebody's attic. But, then, isn't everything in the displays from somebody's attic—or barnyard?" She shrugged. "Sorry, but I'm drawing a complete blank right now. Maybe I'll think of it later."

"That's all right," Shelbie said. "I imagine there was a tag on it at one time, with the number, but it's been lost."

"Could be. But do you want to leave it here for a bit? In case it jogs my memory?"

"No," Shelbie said hastily, not sure why she reached out for the figure so rapidly. Then, in search of a reason, she glanced at the litter surrounding the typewriter. "Would it be safe?" she asked with a grin that was slightly less than genuine.

Marge looked around, not only at the table but at the similarly disorganized bookcases along one wall and the magazines and papers on most of the chairs. "Probably not," she admitted, laughing. "If it didn't get lost by itself, Huntzie would probably think it was a new toy, and you'd get tooth marks all over it. Whatever it is." She looked at the figure again as she handed it back to Shelbie. "God, but it is *ugly!* Looks like one of those Easter Island things with a bad case of acromegaly."

Shelbie nodded as she stood up. "A similar thought occurred to me."

Marge shuddered. "Can you imagine one of those things twenty feet high? Or meeting the model for it walking around? Makes Rondo Hatton look like Mr. America." She held out her hand to Matt as they all three moved back through the kitchen toward the door.

"Nice meeting you, Matt," she said, giving his hand a solid shaking, then looked toward Shelbie. "As long as I'm in the middle of my gossip column for the *Bugle*—and desperate for material, I might add—are you sure I can't enter you two as an item?"

"Come on, Marge!" A touch of annoyance entered Shelbie's voice, but she wondered for a moment if she wasn't overreacting, as she often had the last year or so.

Marge held her hands up defensively. "No offense, Shel, no offense meant. Just doing my thing, which happens to be a gossip column at this particular instant. Okay, if I can't get that kind of a scoop, how about something else? Matt, you moved out of here a long time ago, you and your whole family. What are you doing coming back now? Vacation? Slumming? Getting nostalgic?"

"Nothing wildly newsworthy," he said. "Just trying to get my uncle's estate straightened out. You know how lawyers are."

"Your uncle's estate . . ." Marge stopped, her face thoughtfully suspicious. "Your uncle wouldn't be—have been Ben Cunningham, would he?"

Matt nodded but said nothing. Marge grinned knowingly at Shelbie. "I thought the name sounded familiar. You could do a lot worse than this guy, Shel. If that house his uncle lived in is any indication—" She looked back at Matt, a different kind of appreciation showing in her eyes. "You *did* inherit some of his goodies, didn't you?"

Unexpectedly, he laughed. "We're supposed to, my mother and I. As far as we know, we're the only surviving relatives."

Marge eyed him speculatively. "Just out of pure prying curiosity, how much was he worth? I often wonder about these people who live in big, fancy houses, if they're really as rich as we peasants think."

Matt shrugged. "It's hard to tell. They still don't have everything straightened out. Which is, as I said, why I'm here."

Marge nodded thoughtfully, her eyes still on Matt. "You mean he *didn't* have much? Is that maybe why he killed himself? He was really in debt, and nobody around here knew about it? How about an exclusive story for the *Bugle?* 'Rich Recluse Actually Debt-Ridden,' something along those lines."

Matt started to shake his head, but he stopped, a faint look of puzzlement crossing his face. He glanced toward Shelbie, then looked back at Marge.

"I don't know about his being debt-ridden," he said slowly, "but there *is* something else that sort of relates to him. If you're interested."

"Am I interested?" She waved a despairing hand toward the typewriter on the dining room table. "Is Rockefeller a capitalist? I'm interested in anything and everything. Believe it or not, this has been a slow week around Elwood, gossipwise."

"All right," Matt said, and even before he spoke, Shelbie had an odd feeling about what he was going to say. "According to the sheriff," he went on, "there's been an epidemic of suicides the last three months."

"Epidemic?" Marge frowned disbelievingly. "What's *that* supposed to mean?"

"It means that, starting with my uncle, Ben Cunningham, there have been five suicides in and around Elwood in the last three months. Normally there aren't—"

As he spoke, Marge's eyes lit up. "I know what you mean," she said excitedly. "I just hadn't— Yeah, there was Joe Harrins two or three weeks ago, and then— Wow, how about that? Maybe I should run an article on it. 'Suicide City! Self-Destruction Stalks Midwest Hamlet!' God knows, I need *something* to hype my circulation. My gossip columns sure aren't doing the job. What do you think, Shel? Would you shell out a quarter for an article like that?"

"I might, but . . ." Shelbie's voice trailed off as a vision of Carla surfaced in her mind once again, bringing with it another irrational dusting of guilt.

"Maybe a whole series," Marge was saying, not noticing Shelbie's momentary withdrawal. "One on each victim. Stretch it out over several issues that way. How many did you say there were, Matt?"

"Five," he said, and then paused. Whether it was because he was uncomfortable with the subject or he was trying for dramatic effect, Shelbie couldn't tell. "Including," he finished, "the one we found today."

"The one you—" Marge's eyes widened. "You're kidding! *You* found a body this morning?" She cast her eyes about the room, spotted a scratch pad on one of the chairs and a pencil on a coffee table. She snatched them up and was heading back to the dining-room table a second later. "Come on back here, the two of you. Give me all the details. I'll do this one first, while it's hot, and then I can do a 'retrospective' piece—or whatever it's called—on the others. Now come on, sit down, tell me all about it. Who was it? How did you two—it *was* the *two* of you, wasn't it?"

Matt nodded as they sat down. "Why don't you tell her, Shelbie? You're really the one who found her. And you knew her."

Marge turned to Shelbie, her pencil poised over the scratch

pad. "Well, one or the other of you tell me before I— Well, Shel?"

Shelbie hesitated. She was still uncomfortable thinking about it, but it was a different kind of discomfort now. Before, at the cottage, it had simply been the shock of finding someone she knew, someone as young as Carla, dead, but now . . . She glanced toward Matt, as if his face could give her a clue to her own feelings, but it was no help. There was a difference to the feeling, but that was all she could tell.

"Well?" Marge prodded, tapping the pencil point on the pad.

"It was Carla Schaeffer," Shelbie said. "Remember, she worked in the museum last spring."

Marge scribbled a couple of words, then looked up, frowning. "Carla? But she was— Why would she do something like that? Carla? I'll be—" She shook her head, and a moment later the scribbling resumed. "Okay, how did you happen to find her?"

With Matt listening expressionlessly, Shelbie explained. "So," she finished a couple of minutes later, "we went out there to check before we came in to ask you about that pewter monstrosity. We just—"

"That's it!" Abruptly the scribbling stopped and Marge's hand slapped the table resoundingly. "I knew it would come back if I gave it a little time!"

"That's what?" Shelbie asked.

"Your pewter thing. I just remembered where it came from. It was part of the junk we got from the Brockman place, from that old trunk of Willy's. Some of his nephews or grand-nephews or something were cleaning out the place about the time I took over the society, and they wondered if I wanted to look through the stuff. You know how that is, Shel—everybody figures their own attic is a treasure trove, but— Anyway, your pewter watchamacallit was one of the things we came across in the trunk. They'd had it stashed in their attic for twenty or thirty years."

"Congratulations," Shelbie said, "but what made you remember *that* all of a sudden?"

"I said I would, didn't I? Actually, it was all this suicide talk that did it."

"Suicide talk?" Matt spoke for the first time in minutes, and his voice seemed oddly tense. "Why should that remind you of it?"

"Simple. And you ought to know about it if anyone should, Matt. Don't you remember Willy? Willy Brockman?"

He shook his head. "If he died that long ago, I was just a kid."

"Yeah, sure, but don't you even remember any stories about him? What about you, Shel? Some historical society president you are if you don't remember Willy Brockman. He was the town recluse before Ben Cunningham took over the job. And he killed himself, just like your uncle, back in—oh, it must've been somewhere around nineteen-fifty."

Matt was silent, and both women turned toward him. "Yes," he said softly as he felt their eyes on him, and Shelbie felt the same odd, indefinable discomfort nudging at her stomach. "Yes, I remember now. But I didn't know he killed himself."

Marge shrugged. "Not a lot of people do. The family hushed it up pretty well. It's okay having a rich uncle who gets a reputation for being a well-traveled hermit, but having one who kills himself—well, it just wasn't the thing to do. Not then—not in their social circles, at least. The family knew about it, but they were the only ones. And the coroner knew, I suppose, but they managed to keep the whole thing pretty quiet. It never got in the paper, so far as I know. I'd never have known anything about it except that someone got chatty while I was digging through that trunk. Sally, I think it was. The wife of the nephew or whatever—someone named Gary, anyway. And he was pretty ticked off, even then. Like it knocked a chip out of their family tree or something." Marge shrugged again. "Anyway, that's why I remembered your little pewter monster."

"And they didn't know what it was?" Matt's voice was still soft, but there was a subdued eagerness in his face, in his eyes.

"Not that I remember," Marge said. "But you could probably ask them. They're still around town somewhere. Just moved into a smaller place a few years ago, when the kids grew up. In fact, that's why they were sorting through everything and getting rid of anything they could. They were getting ready to move."

Matt seemed lost in thought for a moment. "Yes," he said finally, "I may try talking to them."

"Fine," Marge said, "but if you do, be careful what you say. Like I told you, they're still pretty touchy about the suicide part of it. At least they were the last time I talked to them, and if they managed to stay uptight about it that long, they probably haven't changed in the last three or four years."

"Do you have an address for them?" he asked.

"Easy enough to find," Marge said, and managed to extract a phone book from the litter on the table. "Easy enough if I can remember the last name, that is. What was it, now? Gary was his first name, but—" She snapped her fingers and started flipping pages. "Here it is. Gary Marks." She handed the book to Matt.

He looked at it, silently mouthed the address a couple of times, and handed the book back. After a moment's silence, he stood up.

Marge blinked. "That was fast. You going to tackle them right now?"

"I thought I'd try. No point in wasting time." He looked toward Shelbie. "If you don't mind my running out on you this way."

Shelbie hesitated, inexplicably reluctant to miss out on Matt's proposed quizzing of the Marks family. Finally she shook her head. "No, of course not," she said, but still there was that indefinable feeling of discomfort, or perhaps uneasiness, that hovered around her, and for a moment there was an urge to ask Matt if he felt the same thing, if it had anything to do with—

"We're not far from the museum, are we?" Matt was asking. "Close enough for me to walk back to my car?"

"Three or four blocks," Shelbie said. "But I can drive you back, and then—"

"No, that's all right. You go ahead with this." His eyes met hers, and for an irrational moment something told her that he *was* feeling the same thing, whatever it was. "I probably need the exercise anyway," he said, then turned and moved quickly through the kitchen to the door.

"Where are you staying?" Marge called after him. "Just in case I want—" She stopped as the screen door slammed behind him. She started to get up, but then flopped back into the chair and shrugged as she positioned the pencil over the pad once again and looked toward Shelbie.

"Now, where were we? Let's see, you had just found the body. Okay. When had you last seen her? And . . ."

CHAPTER 4

Shelbie grimaced as she climbed out of her Toyota in the parking lot and saw Carson Griggs standing outside the museum door watching her. As always, in recent years, his lanky, almost gaunt six-feet-plus was clothed impeccably in a dark, conservative suit. Today he even had a vest. He looked out of place in the dusty alley, just as he had been out of place in Shelbie's life. Or perhaps it was the other way around. She had been out of place in his life. After all, he was the one who was running confidently for the state senate after a busy year on the city council, and she was the one who was an out-of-work teacher filling in with a virtually nonpaying job with the historical society until something better came along. Which could be soon, she reminded herself, remembering the interview with the Argos school board set for Wednesday evening. Which was, she realized, probably why her ex-husband was here. One last pitch to convince her that she didn't need a job, particularly an out-of-town job, and that he was perfectly willing to take her back at any time.

Shelbie shook her head resignedly and started toward him. Unpleasant tasks are best met head on.

"Hi, C.G.," she greeted him as they met a few yards from the museum door. "What brings you out of your oak-paneled den at this time of day?"

His craggy face was, as always, as inscrutable as he could make it, and his dark, almost black hair was perfectly groomed despite the breeze that ruffled her own light brown tangle. Nervously, she brushed a stray strand back from her forehead, and, as her hand dropped back to her side, took an ineffectual swipe at one of the larger patches of gravel-pit dust that still clung to her faded jeans.

"I heard about Carla," he said, and she could hear, faintly, the so-familiar combination of worry and disapproval. Or perhaps it wasn't there at all, but, expecting it, she supplied it herself.

"And you rushed right over to see how I was holding up," she said with deliberate bluntness. "It shook me a little at the time, but I'm doing fine now, thank you."

He hesitated, and again Shelbie supplied her own interpretation of his action, of the hesitation and of the minuscule movement of his heavy eyebrows. He was puzzled, as he always was when his concern—or overconcern—for her was rejected. Even now, after a year and a half of separation . . .

"I understand Matthew Decker was with you this morning," he said finally, "when you found Carla."

Shelbie almost laughed but managed to restrain herself. "That's right. Now, if that's all you wanted to know . . ." She made a move toward the museum door.

He shook his head, his hand reaching out automatically for her arm. She drew back, and his hand dropped stiffly to his side. "I only have your best interest in mind, Shelbie. You know that." The voice was authoritative now, using the same tones she had heard during his campaign speeches. "You do know that, don't you?"

She gave a long, internal sigh, but the only outward indication Shelbie allowed herself was a brief closing of her eyes. She didn't want to get involved in another discussion, so-called, along those lines. C.G. believed what he said. She had realized long since that he was perfectly sincere in his desire to protect her, but that realization only made things worse. That and the fact that it had been one particular act of protectiveness that had, she was retrospectively sure, tipped the scales toward their getting married in the first place. She had been teaching for several months, and the relationship between the idealistic young teacher and the up-and-coming young newspaper editor had been drifting aimlessly for just as long when, one night as she was leaving a school play rehearsal, a disgruntled ex-student who had flunked out of her English class the previous semester, took after her with a knife. It was beginning to look like rape, at the very least, when C.G. had arrived on the scene. The knife-wielding would-be rapist ended up with a few bruises and an arrest record, while C.G. got out of it with only a slashed jacket and a couple of superficial cuts. Shelbie (in true rescued-damsel fashion, she often told herself later) had collapsed in his arms, and somehow, before she could get her perspective back and look at the whole thing logically, they were married. Or that was the way she saw it in hindsight two or three years later, when the regrets began to set in in earnest and when what had first appeared to be gallantry began to evolve into (be revealed as?) a smothering possessiveness. And when mild suggestions that she would be better off if she quit teaching and devoted herself entirely to her husband's welfare and career turned gradually into requests—and then demands.

"I know," she said quietly.

"Then why—" Griggs stopped, and Shelbie thought she could see the inner annoyance, the puzzlement in his eyes. Then there was a faint sigh of resignation.

"There are," he said, "some things you need to know about Mr. Decker."

"All right, C.G.," she said when he hesitated, as if soliciting her permission to continue, though she knew he would continue regardless of what she said. "What deep dark secrets are there in Matt's past that I need to know? But don't forget that I knew him fairly well in high school."

A trace of a smile momentarily pulled at his lips. "But not well enough to know that he was Ben Cunningham's nephew?"

"So? Come on, C.G., what are you driving at?"

"I just want you to be careful, that's all."

"Careful about what? So far you haven't told me anything at all, let alone something I need to be careful about."

"All right, just facts," he said, and then began enumerating them as if they were points in a debate. "Fact one, Decker and his mother are the sole heirs to Cunningham's estate. Fact two,

Decker was in Elwood about the time of his uncle's alleged suicide. Fact three, Decker has also been in Elwood for four days now. Fact four, Carla Schaeffer just committed suicide using the same method as Decker's uncle. Fact five, Carla Schaeffer worked for Phillip Denniston, the lawyer handling the Cunningham estate. Fact six—and this is the one that makes me feel I must warn you—there is a fairly substantial amount of money and property unaccounted for in the Cunningham estate."

Shelbie had been listening with growing incredulity as he methodically went through his list. "And you're suggesting that Matt had something to do with the death and/or the missing money?" She made a sound just short of being a snort. "Come on, C.G., you're reaching pretty far, even for you, if you're hinting at anything like that. You don't really think Matt had anything to do with his uncle's death, do you? It was suicide, remember? Not murder. In any event, how do you know any money is even missing? And if it really is, why haven't I seen a headline in the *Sentinel?*"

He hesitated, as if debating with himself. Apparently deciding, he said, "I didn't want to get Carla into trouble with Denniston."

Shelbie's eyebrows went up. "So Carla told you about all this? The missing money? The fact that Matt and his mother inherit everything?"

He nodded. "When the will didn't come up for probate, I became curious. But the point is—"

"The point is," she interrupted, glancing at her watch, "you have warned me, I thank you for the concern, and now I really must be getting inside. It's almost twelve-thirty, and Cindy can't go to lunch until I get there."

"Very well," he said quietly. It was obvious that he knew what she was really saying, but he still had no real understanding of why, nor of the basic, unchangeable fact that there could never again be anything serious between them. "Just don't forget," he went on, "if you ever need anything . . ."

"I won't forget, C.G."

Then she was walking past him and pushing through the museum door. Inside, as she let the door close slowly behind her, she noticed that the flat rocks were all stacked loosely in the corner, and she thought briefly of where they would eventually be going. First, of course, was the one they were planning to put on the grave of Emma Whitlaw, the first known white to be buried in Farrell County—*if* they could ever decide for sure where the grave was. One theory said that it was under one corner of the Lakewood Heights Shopping Center parking lot. Another theory was that the grave was only a few hundred yards from the log cabin the historical society was building. Somehow, Shelbie suspected, the final decision would be in favor of the cabin location. The merchants in the shopping center had already made it clear that they would not look kindly on even a relatively small rock mounted in their parking lot, especially one pointing out that the bones of Emma Whitlaw had been moldering there for nearly a hundred and fifty years.

But certainly no one could complain about the marker they were planning for the Mound. The only problem would be to get someone to write a hundred words or so explaining the "Legend of the Mound" on the marker and then getting the mayor and all the rest of the last-minute nitpickers to okay the wording. She would, of course, have similar problems for most of the markers, but that one promised to be the worst. In a way, it was like the Whitlaw marker, only with the Mound marker, it wasn't a problem of conflicting locations but conflicting legends. It seemed that each old-timer had his or her own version, which his or her grandparents had heard from the Indians directly. A benevolent god who assured good crops if he was properly appeased. A malevolent demon who killed anyone who crossed him. The stories ran the gamut in trying to explain what lay under the Mound. Tim Remington even had his own monster-movie version, insisting with a straight face that it was probably a buried spaceship that had crashed there a few thousand years before and that something not unlike H. P. Lovecraft's elder gods still survived inside it, awaiting their chance to emerge and take over the world. The truth, as even Tim would admit in his occasional serious moments, was that the

Mound was probably simply a small Indian burial mound, although it was unusual in that it was the only one in this part of the state. They usually came in clusters. Someday, perhaps the historical society would get enough money together to finance an archaeological dig, or maybe even interest one of the state universities in it. In the meantime, the best they could do was put up a marker and hope that the vandals and/or land developers wouldn't disturb or destroy the gods or demons or bones and beads that rested there.

"It's about time!" Cindy said as Shelbie entered the inner room of the museum. "What's this about Carla? Griggs was just in here, and he said something about her being dead?"

Shelbie nodded. "Apparently suicide."

Cindy pursed her lips in a silent whistle. "Carla Schaeffer? A suicide? I don't believe it! How did she do it?"

"Overdose of sleeping pills, probably. But nothing's definite yet."

Another silent whistle. "Any note? And how do you know it was pills?"

"No note," Shelbie said, "and I don't know for sure. Matt did find an empty prescription bottle, though. And I remember last week when she got the prescription filled. Which reminds me—had *you* talked to her lately?"

"Depends on what you mean by lately. I saw her at the lunch counter in Harmon's about a week ago."

"And?"

Cindy shrugged. "And nothing special. Not that I can remember. We just chatted about the usual things. She was having trouble sticking to her diet, especially sitting next to an underweight glutton like me. She certainly didn't give me any hint about *this!*"

"Did she say anything about her job at Denniston's?"

"Not that I remember. Why?"

Shelbie shook her head. "Just C.G. and his suspicious mind," she said. "It's contagious once in a while."

"Oh? Tell me more."

"There's not much to tell. He was looking for foul play under every rock, that's all."

"What sort of— Murder, you mean? Instead of suicide?"

"Who knows? Denniston was handling the Cunningham estate, and—C.G. *says*—there's some money or something missing. And since Carla worked for Denniston . . ." She shrugged.

"And your ex thought Carla might be connected to the missing money? That's why she killed herself? Or *was* killed?" Cindy gave another silent whistle.

"Now don't you start, too," Shelbie admonished."One wild-eyed crank in town is enough."

"But what about the missing money? What happened to it? If it was old Ben Cunningham, it must have been a lot."

"You knew him?"

"Hardly, but I knew *of* him, the same as you. Who didn't? Elwood's own little rustic Howard Hughes. And then when he killed himself—" Cindy stopped, her eyes widening. "He *did* kill himself, didn't he?"

"As far as I know, yes. Now I told you, don't *you* start! Aren't you already late for lunch?"

Cindy waved away the hint. "I can always eat. In fact, I almost always do," she added, glancing at the Twinkie wrappers in the wastebasket. "Now, about this missing money or whatever. How much is missing?"

"I haven't the faintest idea. If you really want to know, talk to C.G. He's the one who's spreading the rumors. Or starting them, at least. It'll probably turn out to be a few dollars from some petty-cash fund, or a misplaced decimal."

"Maybe I *will* ask him," Cindy said. "I'm certainly not getting any encouragement from you."

"And you're not going to, either."

"Okay, if that's the way you're going to be, I might as well— Hey, I almost forgot. The pewter monstrosity—did you find out anything about it? Did Mrs. Remington remember it?"

"As a matter of fact, she did. It was something she picked up from the Markses. It was in an old trunk that belonged to an uncle of theirs, Willy Brockman."

"What was it, though?"

"That we didn't find out. Just something in the trunk, which means it's at least twenty-five or thirty years old, since that's when Brockman died. Or killed himself, according to Marge."

"*Another* suicide? You're running into another one every time you turn around today."

"I've noticed. Now *there's* something a little more intriguing than a few missing dollars. According to Sheriff Rokane, there have been five suicides in the past three months, practically an epidemic. Starting with Ben Cunningham and ending, we hope, with Carla today."

Cindy frowned. "What's the normal rate for around here?"

"Who knows? But it certainly isn't five every three months."

"No, I wouldn't think so, but . . . Yes, I remember, now. One was the Harrins boy, just last month sometime?"

"That's one of them. And a couple others about the same age. You knew Elvon Baker, didn't you?"

"I know the name, but— Yes, I remember, but I thought it was his father! Are you sure it wasn't?"

"Positive. They've all been about the same age, like Carla." Involuntarily, Shelbie shivered. "Someone like Brockman or Cunningham, it's not such a complete shock, but when they're your own age, or even younger . . ."

Cindy nodded. "I know. I just hadn't realized—" She shook her head. "That was one thing that got to me a little while we were doing that family history research. You remember Mrs. Cole, the secretary of the group?"

"I know her. What about her?"

"Nothing about her," Cindy said, "but one of her relatives— a cousin or something like that—was only about twenty or twenty-one when she did herself in. For no reason at all, just like Carla."

"When was that?"

"I'm not sure," Cindy admitted. "Late forties or early fifties, somewhere in there."

Shelbie frowned as, for a moment, a faint tingle seemed to touch her mind, and she glanced around nervously, half-expecting to see someone walking silently behind her. But there was no one. It was as it had been last night, except that through the windows now, instead of darkness, she could see the trees and the bright blue sky beyond, and the shadows in the corners of the room were only tiny patches of greyness, not caverns of blackness.

"That would've been about the same time," Shelbie found herself saying, "that Brockman killed himself. . . ."

"Could be," Cindy said. "But that's one I never heard of, until you mentioned him. Who was he, anyway? Someone I should know?"

"Not necessarily. From what Marge said, he was our—what did you call him? 'Rustic Howard Hughes'?—before Ben Cunningham took over the job."

"Oh? And they both committed suicide? The atmosphere around here must not be very good for small-town tycoons. Say, do you think there might be an article in that? For the *Quarterly,* I mean?"

"Article? On the suicides? You're starting to sound like Marge."

"Not on the suicides, but on those two rich hermits. If Brockman was really that much like Cunningham— I didn't even know we ever had another one like that around here, and I'll bet a lot of other people didn't, either."

"Could be. But you might run into trouble with Brockman's relatives. According to Marge, they're still touchy about it, even now. They even kept the suicide story hushed up somehow."

"And they're still worried about people finding out?" Cindy shook her head disbelievingly. "Well, it takes all kinds, I guess. Still, it might be worth looking into, don't you agree? We publish enough dull family histories in our illustrious *FCHS Quarterly.* Maybe we could get something a little more interesting in there this way."

"And you're volunteering to do the research? Another day or three at the library and courthouse?"

Cindy shrugged. "Why not? I finished up those dues notices and membership and donation pleas this morning, and . . ."

"And you'd sooner browse through old newspapers and records than type. Right?"

"Wouldn't *you?*"

"That's beside the point," Shelbie said, and she was about to point out that there were at least a dozen other projects that needed doing, including sorting and cataloging the box full of odds and ends donated the week before by the Harrisons. But she didn't. She hesitated for no good reason, and then said, "But if you'd like to spend a couple of hours—no more, mind you!—checking it out after lunch, go ahead. But remember, just two hours. And all you're doing is finding out if there's enough material for an article. You're not researching the entire article."

Cindy looked at her startledly for a moment, then grinned. "In that case," she said, grabbing her purse from the floor next to her desk, "I'm going to lunch immediately, before you change your mind. See you in two or three hours." She was through the archway into the outer room before the last words were out.

For several seconds, Shelbie stood silently as the sound of the outer door clanging shut echoed through the rooms. Then, slowly, just a little uneasily, she opened her purse, drew out the tissue-wrapped pewter figure, and, carefully, almost delicately, unwrapped it.

CHAPTER 5

It was late afternoon when Shelbie looked up from the papers on her desk to see Matt approaching. Quickly, she erased the frown she had intended for Cindy, who still had not come back from the library. His jacket was slung over one shoulder, and the almost-rumpled look he had achieved that morning had progressed considerably. Despite its relative shortness, his brown hair dangled limply over his forehead. He glanced briefly toward the display case holding the pewter figure as he walked past it toward her desk.

Shelbie leaned back in her chair and raised a hand in greeting, and Matt nodded in return. For a moment there was silence, each waiting for the other to speak.

"How did it go with the Markses?" Shelbie asked finally. "That *was* where you took off to in such a hurry, wasn't it?"

"It wasn't quite a total disaster," he said, shaking his head, "but it was close enough to last until the real thing comes along. Which, in a way, is one reason I'm here."

"Oh? To tell me you bombed out? The way you dashed out of Marge's place, I figured you wouldn't take no for an answer."

A rueful smile crossed his broad face. "I didn't intend to, but . . . I made the initial mistake of talking to someone besides Sally, and the answer I got was 'Go away and don't bother us any more.' Worded a bit more politely, but that was the idea."

"They denied knowing anything about the pewter monstrosity?"

"Oh, Judith admitted—she was the only one there; Gary was at his office, and Sally was on a shopping trip out of town—

Judith admitted the thing existed and that they had given it and a trunk full of other odds and ends to the historical society a few years back, but that was it. They knew nothing—but *nothing*—about what it might have been or where Uncle Willy might have gotten it. And they wondered if that 'terrible Remington woman' was still associated with the society."

Shelbie laughed. "What did you tell her?"

"That Mrs. Remington was no longer with the society and that she had been replaced by a perfect jewel of a young woman."

"Well, thank you—I think. You were never that fast with a compliment in high school that I can recall." She paused a moment, studying him. "But to tell the truth, that compliment has all the earmarks of a setup of some kind. What are you after, Matt?"

He blinked, surprised at the sudden question. "How could you tell?"

"Don't worry about it," Shelbie told him. "After a year and more in the society, you get to the point where you recognize and use—especially use—every possible approach to a con job. So, as I said—what can I do for you, Matt?"

His laugh was just the slightest bit uncomfortable. "I should've known better. I never was very good at that sort of thing. I'm sorry."

"Don't worry about it. But you really ought to get Marge to give you a lesson or two before you tackle someone again. But, not to lose the original subject altogether, I'm still assuming you have something you'd like me to do for you?"

"As a matter of fact, I do. A sort of continuation of what we started earlier."

"The pewter monstrosity?"

He nodded. "Marge said that if anyone could get some information out of the Markses, you could."

"Don't bet on it. Besides, what makes you think they know any more than they've already told you?"

"I don't know. Maybe they don't. But it's the only—only lead I've got."

"Lead? Lead to what? That pewter thing? Why are you so interested in it?"

He shrugged uncomfortably, looking away for a moment, toward the display case. "For one thing," he said, "it's just a feeling. I can't explain it. It's just that when I see the thing . . ." His voice trailed off.

"And that's all? Just a hunch? Aren't you letting yourself get sidetracked from doing what you came here for?"

He looked at her blankly for a moment before comprehension came. "Oh, the estate, you mean." He shrugged, glanced again toward the display case.

"Yes," Shelbie said, "that would seem to be the first order of business, if it's anywhere near as large as people around here think it is. Incidentally," she went on innocently, remembering the wild suspicions C.G. had forced on her a few hours before, "what's holding things up? Trouble with the will?"

"Darned if I know," he said, sounding relieved to be off the subject of the pewter figure. "Or rather, I know what the problem is, but I haven't the foggiest idea what to do about it."

"And the problem is . . . ?"

"The first problem is, there's no will, but that's easy enough to work out. My mother and I are the only known relatives, and nobody's looking too hard for any distant cousins. The real problem is, most of the estate is missing."

At least, Shelbie thought, he wasn't hiding the problem. "Missing?" she asked. "You mean he lost it before he died? Bad investments?"

"Nothing that simple," he said. "It's just—missing. Frankly, it sounds insane to me, but a few weeks before he died—killed himself—he had everything he could lay his hands on converted into cash. Often at a loss." He paused, looking away again. "And now nobody can find the cash."

"But why—"

"That's what I've been asking ever since I found out about it. And so have the lawyers, believe me. And so far, nobody's come up with any answers. The money—close to half a million, they tell me—is just plain *gone!*"

"But there must be records, something!" A half million, missing? C.G. hadn't said it was *that* much. Shelbie had trouble imagining half a million dollars all in one lump, let alone imagining it being somehow mislaid.

"Not a thing," Matt said. "Everything was converted into as much cash as he could get—literally—and delivered to him. What happened to it after that—" He held his hands out sideways, palms up, and hunched his shoulders in a broad shrug. "It just vanished. For all anybody's been able to learn, he could have dumped it in an incinerator in his basement."

"But that doesn't make sense!"

"You're telling me? I arrived at that same conclusion about two months ago, all of half a second after Denniston worked up the nerve to tell me about it." A grin broke through as he added, "And he spent the next half hour agreeing emphatically and assuring me that his firm had done absolutely nothing irregular and that he was even more puzzled and troubled than I was."

"You believed him?"

"Why not? If they'd wanted to skim something off the top, aside from the usual outrageous probate fees, there were a hundred ways of doing it that I'd never have noticed. No, I can't imagine them trying to pull anything like that."

"You don't seem too worked up about it. If I lost a half million, I'd probably be doing a lot of screaming."

"What good would that do? Besides, I went through that stage a couple of months ago. You should've heard me scream then! And after the screaming, I hired another lawyer and had him go over every scrap of paper he could find that had anything to do with my uncle. I even hired a private detective, for all the good it did. Which was zilch."

"They didn't find anything?"

"Absolutely zero. For all we know, Uncle Ben decided to take it with him, and then found a way to really do it. Except that he didn't have any reason to go in the first place, and that makes even less sense." He shook his head. "So you see, I haven't been exactly resigned about the whole thing. But at this point, I'm at a loss as to what to do next. Other than to do my best to laugh at the whole thing and to grasp any straws or hunches that happen to wander by."

"What about blackmail?" Shelbie asked, and then continued with objections to her own suggestion before he could answer. "Although I can't imagine anything that would be worth a half million to cover up."

"I thought of it, believe me. That's one of the things the detectives looked into. And it makes as much sense as anything else, especially when you consider that he killed himself only a week or two after he got the last of the cash in his hands. As you say, I can't imagine anything being that horrendous, especially to a hermit like him. But I suppose it's possible. Maybe he paid the blackmailer all the money he could lay his hands on, and then the blackmailer threatened to expose him anyway. So he killed himself."

"Nice and neat. Neat, anyway. But . . ."

"I know. But impossible. In any event, the detectives couldn't find a trace of anything or anybody." Decker shrugged again. "So there you are. Or there *I* am, rather. I've spent a couple thousand of my own money, and I'm nowhere."

"But you're back here now. And this morning you said you were here to 'straighten out your uncle's estate.'"

"Euphemistically speaking." He laughed, and perhaps there was a touch of bitterness in the laugh this time. "What I'm really doing is spending a couple weeks of my vacation here, wasting my time on hunches and clutching at straws. You know how you always figure the guy you hired *must* have overlooked something or done something wrong, and that you can certainly do better if you only get in there yourself . . ."

Shelbie was silent as Matt's voice trailed off and his eyes moved around the room again, eventually touching the display case and the pewter figure.

"And the pewter monstrosity is one of your hunches?" she asked.

He continued to look at the figure for a moment, then turned back to Shelbie. "My uncle had one just like it," he said.

Abruptly, without warning, the feeling that had touched her the night before swept over her once again. But this time it was stronger, much stronger.

And different.

The night before, it had been an uneasiness verging on fear, the kind of feeling that comes so often in darkened rooms and hallways; the feeling that, if only you could somehow see behind yourself without actually having to turn around, there would be someone—or something—there.

But now . . .

There was the sense of a presence, but somehow it was not the same. There was uneasiness but not fear, not even apprehension. But perhaps that was because she was not alone now, perhaps because the light from the afternoon sun still struck the trees beyond the windows, perhaps because . . .

Then, as suddenly as it had come, the feeling was gone.

It was only when she felt the air flowing out between her slightly parted lips with a faint whooshing that she realized she had been holding her breath for several seconds and that Matt was moving toward her, frowning.

"Are you all right?" he asked as he moved around the desk to where she was sitting. He put a hand on her shoulder.

"Yes," she said quickly. "Yes, I'm fine." She stood up and moved away from him around the desk. "I'm fine."

She found herself at the display case, looking down at the pewter figure. As she heard Matt moving up behind her, she drew another quick breath and turned toward him.

"You were saying your uncle had one of these things? Was his as ugly as this one?"

He hesitated as he stood in front of her, his broad forehead still creased in a frown. "You're sure you're all right? You looked for a second there as if you were going into a trance."

"I'm all right!" she snapped, then shook her head. "I'm sorry. I didn't mean to sound like that, but—I am all right, though. Okay?"

"Okay," Matt said after a moment. The frown faded, but his

eyes still reflected concern. He looked past her then, into the display case again.

"As far as I know," he said, "the one my uncle had was identical to this. Although my memory of it probably isn't all that accurate. I saw it only a couple of times, and I couldn't have been more than five or six at the time."

"What happened to it?"

He shrugged. "It may still be around, for all I know. Unless that's one of the things he sold."

"You didn't find it while you were searching for the money?"

"I wasn't looking for it then," he said. "There were the usual trunks and boxes, but— Come to think of it, though, Denniston and his crew did do a complete inventory last month. So if it's still around, they probably listed it. Unless it's part of something like 'Odds and ends, one box of.' I can't imagine even a complete inventory listing each and every knickknack and paperweight separately."

"But maybe whoever did the inventory would remember it?"

He glanced at the figure, grimacing. "I would think so. I've remembered it nearly twenty-five years." He looked back at Shelbie. "Do you suppose I—we—could take it around to the appraisers and ask them?"

"I don't see why not," she said after a moment's hesitation. "If Cindy ever gets back from the library, that is." She glanced at her watch. "Which is looking less and less likely."

"Would you want me to go look for her?"

"No need. But now that you bring up the thought of looking for her, I think I will give the library a call." She shook her head. "Usually she's fairly reliable. She must've found something pretty interesting."

"Oh? What was she looking for?"

"Actually, it's vaguely related to that thing," she said, indicating the pewter figure. "And maybe to your own quest this afternoon. We were talking about doing an article about Brockman for the society's quarterly magazine, and she was going to check through the newspapers from about the time he died, just to see if he sounded interesting enough."

"Perfect," Matt said. "If you're going to do an article like that, then you'll have the perfect excuse to talk to the Markses, won't you?"

"Well, an excuse, at any rate. If you haven't already alienated them completely. But that wasn't all the article was going to be about. Since Brockman was the local rich recluse before your uncle took over the job, we'd probably want to cover both of them. Or do you have some objections to having part of an article written about your uncle?"

He shook his head. "None at all. It should certainly be more . . . dignified than whatever Marge is coming up with. And if you would care to question me about him over dinner to-night . . . ?"

She hesitated a moment as Carson Griggs's suspicions darted through her mind, but she dismissed them quickly. If anyone had grounds for suspicion, it was Matt, not C.G. After all, he was the one who seemed to have been done out of a half million dollars.

"All right," she said, "I'll bring my cassette recorder. Okay?"

"Sure. And I—" He stopped as the outer door slammed back noisily, and a moment later Cindy appeared in the archway to the other room.

"It's about time," Shelbie began, but Cindy, raising her hands in a "hold it" gesture, interrupted.

"You'll never guess what I found!"

"Probably not," Shelbie said, "since I don't intend to try. Now, Cindy—"

"There was *another* epidemic! In nineteen fifty-one!" Cindy looked from Shelbie to Matt and back, her eyes sparkling.

"Another epidemic of what?" Shelbie asked, but even as she did, the knot in her stomach was telling her that she already knew the answer.

"Of suicides—what else? I wasn't sure just when Brockman died, so I had to skim back through the papers, you know, for the obituaries they always have on the last page. Well, I found it, eventually, but before I did— You're not going to believe this, but there were six—*six*, mind you, all in a four-month period! That relative of Mrs. Cole, remember? She was one of them. The third, I think. And every one was young—early twenties or late twenties at the oldest. *Every one!"*

Shelbie barely heard her. As Cindy had begun talking, rapidly, animatedly, the feeling of a presence had flowed over Shelbie once again, just as it had only minutes before. Involuntarily, she moved away from the display case, half-afraid that if she looked into it, the vacant, shadowed eyes of the pewter figure would be following her.

But then, even more quickly than it had come, it was gone, leaving in its wake only a faint feeling of shock.

What was going on? This wasn't like her, not at all, Shelbie told herself severely. She wasn't the type to get sudden chills or intuitions or anything else like that, and for a moment—just a moment—the stomach-churning idea of insanity darted through her mind. Insanity of the sort that must have driven Carla to—

Shelbie shook her head sharply, bringing herself back to the present again. This time no one had noticed her brief lapse. Matt was intently questioning Cindy, who was still on the high she had gotten from her discovery.

"What about Brockman?" Matt was asking. "Where did he fit into your epidemic?"

"The first. At least, I couldn't find anyone earlier, and I checked back almost a year. Oh, I found one other suicide, but that was a middle-aged guy, and his wife had died a few months before. And he was eight or nine months before Brockman, anyway."

"And the dates? Do you remember them exactly?"

Cindy shook her head. "But I wrote them all down," she said, digging a half dozen file cards from her purse. "Brockman —that was on, let's see . . . Here it is. April twenty-eighth. And the next one, William Hartford, was May fifteenth. Then June twentieth, that was Sheila Raymond. Mrs. Cole's relative, remember? Then Arthur Radtke on July tenth, although they didn't find the body until the fifteenth, so they weren't completely sure about the date. Then August fifth was John Sharp, and August twentieth was Herbert Corlie. And that was it. Four months and six suicides. And no reason for *any* of them!"

Matt was frowning puzzledly. "And no one got suspicious?"

"I guess nobody even noticed," Cindy said. "At least, there wasn't anything mentioned about it in the papers I looked at. But what about the current epidemic? There've been five already, haven't there? And I haven't heard anyone say a word until today. But now that we know this, should *we* do something?"

"What *can* we do?" Shelbie found herself asking, and they both turned to look at her. "The sheriff already knows about them. He's the one who told me, remember? And he isn't— well, he's taking it seriously enough, but only because his own daughter is just the right age to be the next suicide. But what can he *do* about it? Besides keep a close eye on his daughter."

"We could tell him about the other epidemic," Cindy said, her voice starting to sound uncertain.

"And if we do," Matt said, "what's he going to do about it? Start looking for some nut who thinks he's Jack the Ripper, only he specializes in suicides?"

"Of course, if all you want to do is publicize it," Shelbie said, "we can tell Marge about it. She's already planning a series on the current batch. She'd love to get her hands on something like this second one."

Cindy looked at the two of them. "What you're saying is, we can't really do *anything*. Nothing worthwhile, at any rate."

She was coming down from the triumph of her discovery. At first it had been an adventure, Shelbie knew, much the same kind of adventure that searching through old trunks and attics was for Shelbie. But now reality was intruding. In the same way that Shelbie often realized that the trunks and attics represented people's lives, Cindy was beginning to realize—*really* realize— that the names she had been reading about had been people, real people. And that whatever it was she had discovered could still be going on. And that she was powerless to stop it.

"You're probably right," Matt said softly, and Shelbie realized that the mood had overtaken him as well. "We'll tell the sheriff, of course, but it won't mean anything."

There was a silence then, and Shelbie could hear the street noises in the distant afternoon. They seemed unreal now, divorced somehow from the strange reality of the three of them standing there, from the reality of the deaths that still floated in the air around them.

No, Shelbie thought, it *won't* mean anything.

Until the next death . . .

CHAPTER 6

Shelbie called Sheriff Rokane, and it went about as she had anticipated. He sounded both irritated and frightened, no matter how much he tried to conceal it, and Shelbie's theory about his daughter seemed confirmed. He was frightened for Joan and irritated because he could do nothing about it. Or perhaps he was irritated because he couldn't fully convince himself that the whole idea of "suicide epidemics" was sheer nonsense, and the last thing he needed now was more evidence that they were real after all. When Shelbie mentioned Marge and her *Bugle* series, his irritation flared, and he told her he didn't need that kind of aggravation and that he would greatly appreciate it if Marge didn't find out about the alleged 1951 epidemic. "All we need is a story like that, and half the people in the county will be scared out of their wits. And there are probably one or two out there who are just impressionable enough to go off the deep end and actually try to kill themselves."

After the phone call to the sheriff, there was really nothing else any of them could think to do, and eventually Matt left, saying he'd pick Shelbie up for dinner in a couple of hours. Cindy, temporarily depressed by the turn of events, started typing up the government forms that Shelbie had been working on for the last two weeks and had finally completed that afternoon. Shelbie, after finding herself staring blankly toward the pewter figure for the third time, made a lame excuse to Cindy and left a half hour early.

There were, of course, plenty of things that she could have been doing—*should* have been doing, she told herself as she drove—but she felt oddly at a loss, unable to concentrate on anything. There were a half dozen people she should phone to check on their furniture donations for the log cabin being built —old rocking chairs, oil lamps, even a spinning wheel. And there were a couple of families who supposedly owned some authentic-looking logs that could be used in the cabin construction. Arrangements had to be made to haul them into town. And there was the speech she had promised to give to one of the local women's clubs, and she hadn't even started the research on that. She had a good idea of what the subject was going to be—some of the more notable women in Farrell County's history—but so far all she had accumulated were a half dozen names and discouragingly few facts. And there were the—

Shelbie shook her head and jammed on the brakes as she realized she had come within a few feet of driving right past her own house. This was getting to be too much, she thought irritably, definitely too much. First there were those "feelings" popping out of thin air, and now her mind was wandering so aimlessly that she had almost missed her own house.

Even in her apartment, things did not get better. A hot bath, which usually relaxed her when all else failed, gave her only a momentary euphoria as she slid into the steamy water. The sense of relaxation was gone before she could more than lean her head back against the end of the tub. Soon she was scrubbing vigorously, rushing through one of the few things she invariably did at a leisurely pace these days, no matter what the pressures. It was as if she were hurrying toward some unseen goal even though she had no idea what that goal might be. Certainly it wasn't her "date" with Matt, although she did have to admit that she was looking forward to it even if it was at least part business. Despite C.G.'s outlandish suspicions—or perhaps, perversely, because of them?—she felt oddly relaxed about Matt, which was, now that she thought about it, unusual in itself. There were, first, the inexplicable "feelings" that had been assaulting her at odd moments since last night. But even disregarding those, Shelbie had not felt completely at ease with any man since the breakup with C.G. Occasionally she asked

herself why, and occasionally she even answered herself in various ways, saying that perhaps she just didn't want to rush into
anything the way she had the first time, that she didn't want to
commit herself to anything until she could know for *sure* what
a man was like. But usually she simply kept busy and avoided
the problem altogether.

But now . . .

For one thing, she told herself logically, Matt was not a
stranger. She had known him in high school, had even had
what might have been called a "crush" on him for a short
while. For another, the dinner tonight wasn't strictly a date,
anyway. She would have the cassette recorder along and would
be quizzing him about his late uncle. And they would undoubtedly spend some of the time speculating about the rashes of suicides, no matter how much they might try to avoid the subject.

The suicides . . .

Despite the temperature of the water and the vigorous scrubbing, Shelbie felt a faint chill spread over her as she remembered the last time she had seen Carla alive. They had met
briefly on the street, and Shelbie had commented on how tired
Carla had looked, and Carla had told her about the dreams—
nightmares—although she hadn't said what they were about,
only that they were constantly waking her up, and—what was it
she had said? Something about voices? Voices in the dreams
that wouldn't let her sleep . . .

Shelbie climbed out of the tub, dried herself roughly, and
dressed, forcing herself to take her time, lingering over the
choice of blouse and slacks, something she rarely did under
normal circumstances. She even spent a few minutes experimentally poking her hair this way and that, which was obviously a lost cause from the start. The best she could hope for
without professional help was a pleasantly informal, tousled
look. But all the while, as she tried on different items of cloth-
ing, different earrings—which she normally didn't wear at all—
different ways of brushing her hair, it was as if she were trying
to hold herself to an easy stroll while a powerful wind gusted at

her back, urging her on. But urging her on toward what? There was nothing but—

Then, like the other feelings, both last night and today, it was gone, and for a moment there was a faint feeling of loss, perhaps of futility, and she couldn't completely block out the memory of Carla, who must certainly have felt futility when she—

Irritably, Shelbie threw herself down in a chair by a west window, still filled with the late afternoon sun, and picked up a mystery novel she had been intending to read for the past two weeks but had never gotten around to. It was good—the latest by Sjöwall and Wahlöö—but by the time Matt arrived, she had gotten through only two chapters and would have had a hard time giving anyone more than a rough idea of what it was about. The only thing that kept cropping up in her mind was the fact that there would be no more books by the Swedish couple because Per Wahlöö had died last summer at the age of only forty-nine.

During the drive to the lake, Shelbie and Matt avoided both uncles and suicides, largely because of Matt's conversation piece of a car. It was a Checker of indeterminate age, and it somehow seemed to fit Matt, both physically and mentally. The Checker had the same body style it had had since at least the mid-fifties and therefore never went out of style, largely because it had never been in style to begin with. The suit Matt wore—plain and brown—was no more in fashion or out of fashion than the car, and even his general appearance matched it to a degree. His broad, solid build was just a trifle broader than necessary in the middle, and the solidness was the rounded-at-the-edges type rather than the sharp, rippling type that flexed at the beaches every summer. Solid, unspectacular, seemingly reliable, totally unlike C.G., who, now that she thought about it, also matched the car he drove—a Mercedes —at least in some ways.

From their table at the Lakeview, most of the lake was visible through the one wall, made almost entirely of glass, and as they watched, the last remnants of redness faded above the trees

on the opposite shore. Here and there, lights came into existence, and as they did, Shelbie's mind was pulled back to the
subjects they had so far avoided, almost forgotten. Somewhere
across the water, she knew, despite the fact that there were no
lights to mark it, was Carla's cottage.

When the waitress left with their orders, Shelbie dug into her
purse and came out with the miniature cassette recorder, set it
to record, and placed it on the table in front of Matt.

"All right," she said, "just to get the business out of the way
—tell me about your uncle."

He looked at the recorder for a moment, then shrugged. "As
I think I said already, there's not much I can tell you. The last
time I saw him was"—he hesitated, as if trying to remember—
"was twenty-three years ago."

"But you must know *something* about him," she said when
he fell silent again.

"Probably less than the people who live around here. In fact,
I'm sure of it. When the question of the missing money came
up first, one of the things the detectives did was talk to everyone who had known him around here."

"And?"

"And they didn't find out much, but what little they did find
out was more than I had known."

"Which isn't very helpful, if you don't mind my saying so."

He shrugged again. "I can give you the detectives' reports, if
that will help you any. But it all boils down to the fact that he
had no close friends around here, and few acquaintances.
There was an occasional mistress—or some woman staying
with him for no other known reason, at any rate. And he trav-
eled a lot."

"And his wealth? That's always a fascinating subject for
most people who don't have any themselves."

"Nothing spectacular there, either. Real estate around the
state. Stocks. Bonds. Whatever required the least amount of su-
pervision on his part and provided an adequate income."

"And the source? How did he originally make his money? Or
did he inherit it?"

"No idea. There just aren't any records, financial or otherwise, more than eight or ten years old. However far back the IRS statute of limitations goes, that's roughly how far back his records go. Beyond that . . ." He shrugged again.

"But you—or your parents—must have known where the money came from. A half million, or however much he had then, doesn't just appear out of thin air."

"It doesn't?" A touch of bitterness entered his voice. "I remember practically nothing myself, of course, but I asked my mother—Ben's sister—often enough. Either she's not talking, or she doesn't remember any more than I do. One year he took off on a trip, and the next year, he bought that house. He must've stumbled onto some fabulous get-rich-quick scheme during that trip—that's all anyone's ever been able to figure. Or he saved some grateful millionaire's life. But whatever it was, he never told anyone—anyone that I've been able to find, at least."

Shelbie pursed her lips in a silent whistle. "Now, *that* is interesting. I guess we weren't that far off when we called him a local Howard Hughes. But even with Hughes, people knew where the money came from. There must've been *some* indication. What about tax returns?"

"As I said, there are none from that far back—not in his files, at least. Maybe the government has them in an IRS vault or computer somewhere, but getting them is another story. Besides, the problem is not where the money came from twenty-odd years ago, but where it went to three months ago."

"Unless it was just a loan," Shelbie said, "maybe from that theoretical millionaire whose life he saved. In which case the money is back where it came from."

He looked at her blankly for a moment before he realized she wasn't serious. "Sure," he said, "or maybe he sold his soul to the devil for a half million twenty-five years ago, and he had to give them both up."

Shelbie smiled at the idea, but the mention of the devil brought the pewter figure back to mind. Or back to the *surface* of her mind, she realized, for it had never really been completely gone—just temporarily submerged. She started to reach for the cassette recorder.

"Through?" Matt asked.

She hesitated, leaving the recorder going. "From what you say, there's not much point in trying to pursue it any further. Unless you *do* have something more to tell me about your uncle. . . ."

He shook his head. "I wish I could help, but I just don't know that much. And if my mother knows any more, she's not talking."

"And your own memories? Nothing at all?"

"You know how people remember things from that age. He didn't make much of an impression, apparently. Not as much as that pewter figure, whatever it was. Or is. He was just a nice 'older man'—almost as old as I am now, come to think of it, a decrepit thirty."

"What about his job? What did he do before he came into that money?"

"I don't know. I suppose he must've had some kind of job, but . . . Nothing fabulous, I'm sure. The house he lived in seemed big to me at the time, but I took a look at it last week, and it's pretty small. Four rooms, out at the north end of town. Not even in a good neighborhood, as Elwood neighborhoods go."

Shelbie shook her head. "And yet he made a half million dollars somehow. But what about hobbies? He must've had something to keep himself occupied between trips, and you said he never did much to look after his investments."

"A woman now and then, apparently; always someone he brought back with him from the trips, according to the detectives. And planning for more trips. And reading, if the size of the library is any indication."

"Library? His private library, you mean?"

Matt nodded. "Not quite as big as the local public library, but not far from it. It hasn't been totally inventoried, of course, but they're guessing at thirty to forty thousand items of one kind or another."

Shelbie's eyebrows went up appreciatively. "No wonder he needed a large house. What sort of books? Was he a reader or a collector?"

"Probably a reader. There certainly wasn't much point in collecting the things he had."

"Oh? Such as?"

"I don't know everything that's in there, but I did glance through it last week again, and I spotted bits and pieces of everything. Histories, biographies, all kinds of novels, a fair amount of science—the *Science News* and *Scientific American* variety, nothing really deep or technical. Even a few dozen UFO and occult books, and some of the UFO magazines. Like I said, you name it, he probably had at least a sample of it."

"It sounds fascinating," Shelbie said, realizing that her repressed urge for exploring unknown houses was reasserting itself with a vengeance. It had surfaced briefly when she had first learned who Matt's uncle had been, but the events of the day had, until now, kept it subdued.

"I don't intend to sound pushy," she went on, "but is there a chance of getting a tour of that library? And the rest of the place? As I told you this morning, your uncle's place and a half dozen others around town have frustrated me for years."

Matt laughed, apparently back in good spirits.

"Sure. When would you like the guided tour? How about tonight?"

She started to shake her head and say that it would be better to do it by daylight, but she didn't. Instead, she looked out across the lake toward the opposite shore where, somewhere amid the darkness and occasional sparkles of light, she knew the house stood waiting.

"All right," she said. "And don't forget," she added, pointing at the still-running cassette, "your offer is recorded."

He nodded, grinning, and leaned toward the machine. "And tomorrow you promise to worm what you can out of the Markses—and show that pewter figure to the inventory people. Right?"

"Right."

She turned off the recorder and dropped it into her purse. Briefly she thought of the seemingly endless list of things she should be doing for the historical society, even wondered if there wasn't something she should really be doing to prepare for the job interview at Argos the next evening, but neither thought lasted more than a moment. She knew that, until more of her curiosity was satisfied, she wouldn't be able to concentrate on the society's business anyway. And there was really nothing she *could* do to prepare for the interview. School boards either liked you or they didn't, and the only preparation you could do was worry a lot, which only made matters worse. So she might as well continue to indulge her curiosity—her feelings?—while she could.

The house—mansion, really—was set back at least a hundred yards from the winding blacktop road. In the daylight, parts of the house would be visible through the trees, but now, with a half moon in the sky, there was only blackness. Matt turned the car into the narrow drive and stopped before the high iron gate that stood between two concrete pillars.

"No mastiffs guarding the portals," he said as he climbed out to unlock the gate, "but that's about all that's missing."

The gates swung back with only a slight creaking, and Matt maneuvered the Checker through. Ahead of them, at the end of the tunnel through the trees, sections of the house came into sight and grew in the headlights as they approached. It was not so much large as it was massive, Shelbie thought. There was none of the ornamentation or gingerbread that went with most such houses. Instead, it was stark and plain. The walls, brick and masonry, were flat and square, and only a half dozen widely spaced windows kept it from looking like a gigantic blockhouse. A wide built-in garage took up several yards of the ground level at the left. Matt parked the Checker in front of the garage doors, its headlights pointed toward the large, unornamented door set in the center of the front of the house at the top of a short flight of steps.

They sat for a minute after the headlights were turned off,

letting their eyes adjust. In the shadowy moonlight, the house looked even blockier, more austere.

"Should've brought a flashlight," Matt said as they finally climbed out and walked slowly across the lawn to the front door. "But, then, I wasn't expecting to be conducting tours tonight . . ."

He held the ring of keys close to his face, selected one, and inserted it in the lock. The door swung open easily, and light flooded the entire front of the house as Matt located the switches just inside the door. Shelbie squinted as she looked around and located the two bare bulbs mounted on miniature street lamp posts a few yards out from each corner of the house.

As lights came on inside, she saw that the interior was as plain as the outside. On the left was a broad arch leading into what looked like a living room, and on the right was a closed door. Just beyond the door toward the back of the house, a straight flight of stairs disappeared into the shadows of the second floor. A couple of paintings—nondescript landscapes— were on the walls of the living room, and another was in the hallway they were standing in, but that was all. The walls themselves were plain, painted a depressing dark green, and the furniture—the couches and chairs and occasional tables—were the sort of thing that could be found in any local furniture store. Whatever Ben Cunningham had spent his money on, it apparently had not been expensive or exotic furniture. Not in these rooms, at least.

"The library's through here," Matt said, pushing open the door on the right and flipping on a light. "Part of it, at least. There's another room just like it upstairs."

Shelbie whistled silently, as much in envy as anything else. The ceilings were high—at least ten feet—and every square foot of wall space was covered with glass-fronted, floor-to-ceiling bookshelves, all nearly completely filled. And with only one window and two doors in the room, there was lots of wall space. As Matt had said, the assortment was varied. There were none of the "uniformly bound editions" that usually sat unread on the shelves of most private libraries of this size, nor were there any particularly expensive-looking bindings in evidence. Instead, hardcovers of all shapes and sizes were mixed in with paperbacks and magazines. None looked dog-eared or disintegrating from repeated use, but neither could she find any that were obviously untouched, in mint condition.

Once they got around to it, the rest of the house was anticlimactic. There were the usual number of living rooms, guest rooms, etc., that went with large old houses such as this, but there was also a small, heated swimming pool and a sauna in the basement, as well as a game room with not only pool tables, but a half dozen pinball machines. Above the built-in garage were comfortable quarters for a cook and housekeeper. There were no old trunks in the attic. In fact, there was not even an attic. Apparently nothing, once used, was ever saved, aside from the two rooms full of books and magazines.

The only oddity was a single tiny room off the luxurious master bedroom. It was little larger than a walk-in closet, and there were no windows, no openings at all, except for the single, almost completely concealed sliding door. Shelbie shuddered as Matt closed the door behind them for effect. The green—the same disturbing color that dominated the entire interior of the house—made the room seem even more like a cell. The only furniture in the room was a huge reclining chair, seemingly too large to have come through the door. And the only break in the barren walls was a single niche about four feet off the floor, a little arch-topped alcove a foot deep and a little more than that high. Like the rest of the room, it was empty.

"What on earth was *this* for?" Shelbie asked as she leaned hesitantly against the chair.

Matt shrugged. "I have no idea. But whatever it is, it wasn't Uncle Ben's idea. I got a little curious, too, when I saw it the first time, so I tried to look up the last owners, the ones before Uncle Ben."

"And?"

"The only ones I could find were some grandchildren of the owners, but they remembered the room. As far as they knew, it hadn't been used for much of anything. They used to play in it as kids. A great place to hide from the grownups, they said. That was back in the thirties. And it doesn't look like it's the result of remodeling. Whatever it is, it was probably in the house from the start."

"How old *is* this place?"

"Denniston checked into that when he was getting it appraised for the estate, and he said it was originally built in 1885, by one Josiah Wintergreen, a local businessman who made good."

Shelbie shook her head, shivering once again. "Such a strange little room, especially that alcove in the wall." She laughed nervously. "Looks almost like a shrine of some sort. You didn't find any incense in here, did you?"

He shook his head. "Odd you should say that, though. I thought the same thing when I first saw the room."

Another faint shudder. "You don't suppose this is where he kept that pewter monstrosity, do you?"

Matt laughed, but there was a touch of nervousness in the sound. "Sure," he said, "and he came in here and got in a little restful worship once every full moon—if he happened to be home during the full moon, that is. Come on, let's get out of here. I don't know about you, but—"

"Me, too," she agreed quickly, turning toward the door, then experiencing a momentary disorienting panic as she couldn't immediately locate the outline of the door in the dim light. But then it was sliding back under Matt's firm hand, and she breathed a sigh of relief as they stepped back into the master bedroom. The door, counterweighted or spring-loaded, slid shut with a solid, muffled thud.

CHAPTER 7

"Joseph Karns?" The man who answered Shelbie's knock was short, middle-aged, and balding. His shirtsleeves were rolled up, and his expression was vaguely annoyed. In the living room behind him stood a woman, slightly younger and much slimmer, her dark hair tied back in a bun, a clipboard and pencil in her hands.

"Yes? What can I do for you?"

Shelbie introduced herself quickly. "Mr. Denniston said you had done the appraisal of the Cunningham estate," she finished.

"That's right. And now we're trying to do the same for the Carlson estate." His eyes went briefly to the room around him, the impatience plain in his face.

"I won't take any more of your time than I have to," Shelbie said. "I just wanted to ask you about one specific item you may have seen in the Cunningham house."

"If we saw it, it was included in the appraisal," Karns said shortly.

"I'm sure it was," Shelbie said. "But as I understand it, only major items were listed individually. Smaller items were, for the most part, lumped together."

"We couldn't list everything, obviously. That would take weeks. Or years, if we'd tried to catalog all those books."

"Of course. But I'm interested in one specific item, which you probably—"

"That was months ago. I can hardly be expected to remember every little thing we saw."

"I realize that," Shelbie said, opening her purse and reaching for the tissue-wrapped pewter figure she had taken from the museum case earlier in the morning, "but this is something I imagine you would have remembered."

"As I said—" Karns's voice cut off sharply as the tissue was removed from the figure and Shelbie held it out to him. He frowned as he looked down at it briefly. "This is what you were wondering about?" he asked.

She nodded. "Something very much like it, though not necessarily identical."

He shook his head. "Sorry."

"You didn't see it or you don't remember?"

"We didn't see it."

Shelbie glanced toward the woman, who had come forward to look at the figure herself. She had fastened the pencil to the clipboard, which she still held. She grimaced faintly as she looked at the figure in Shelbie's hand.

"Yes," the woman said, "I saw it. Don't you remember, Joe?"

He glanced toward her irritably. "I can't remember everything, not in every house we go through."

She reached out for the figure, and Shelbie let her take it. "You saw it, then?" Shelbie asked. "In the house?"

"Yes, it was a long time ago, but . . ." She looked down at the figure again, then handed it back to Shelbie. "Something like this was in the big bedroom, the one with the big window. It was standing on something, I think."

"On top of the bureau, you mean? Not inside, in a drawer?"

"Something like that. Maybe the table next to the bed. It was out in the open, anyway—I remember that much. I remember wondering what it was at the time." She hesitated and, after a brief glance toward her husband, went on. "What *is* it, anyway?"

Shelbie shook her head. "That's what I'm trying to find out. Just an ugly little figure made out of pewter, so far as I can tell."

"Where did that one come from?"

"Originally from Willy Brockman's estate."

"Brockman . . ." Mrs. Karns shook her head. "Can't place the name."

"He died back in the fifties," Shelbie said, "so it's not surprising you don't remember him. But you said this was in the bedroom in the Cunningham house? Just when was that? When did you make your appraisal?"

"A day or two after Cunningham died. Denniston seemed in an awful rush for some reason. We had to postpone two or three other jobs we had originally scheduled, but he insisted."

Shelbie nodded. It apparently hadn't taken the lawyer long to realize that something was missing. "The figure wasn't removed or put away for any reason, was it? The last you saw of it, it was—"

"Are you accusing us of—" Karns began, but his wife cut him off sharply.

"She's not accusing us of anything, Joe! For God's sake!" She turned back to Shelbie. "I'm sorry about this, but— No, it was out in the open, and if it was removed or put away anywhere, it wasn't done by either of us."

Shelbie nodded, replacing the figure in her purse. "Thank you," she said, keeping her eyes on Karns. "Thank you very much for your help."

"Any time," the woman said.

As Shelbie turned to go down the steps, the door slammed behind her, and she could hear Karns's harsh voice, though she couldn't make out the words.

Sally Marks was one of those women of indeterminate age. She could have said she was sixty or forty, and Shelbie wouldn't have been surprised at either number. Her hair was short, not unlike Shelbie's own, and with touches of grey here and there amid the dark brown. The slacks and sweater she wore were expensive, but looked casual and comfortable.

"My brother was a bit disturbed by your friend yesterday," she said as they settled themselves in the Marks's living room, a rather stiff, formal-looking room that didn't seem to fit Sally Marks at all.

"So I understand," Shelbie said. "That's why I arranged to see you when he and his wife wouldn't be here."

Sally laughed, a light, genuinely amused sound. "Lovely! Now, before he gets back, what was it you wanted to talk about? All Gary did was mutter about somebody coming around and—'prying,' I think was his word. Where *is* your friend, by the way?"

"Looking around his uncle's house again, I think," Shelbie said. "At least, that's where he said he was going when I talked to him a few minutes ago."

Sally nodded. "Now, what can I do for you, now that you've arranged to talk to me without my keepers?"

"This." Shelbie pulled the pewter figure from her purse and set it on the coffee table in front of the couch they were both seated on. Sally crinkled her nose as she looked at the figure.

"That thing! What did you want to know about it? I thought we were through with it when that other woman—what was her name?—took that trunk full of junk away."

"Marge Remington," Shelbie said, and Sally nodded in remembrance. "It's been in the museum since then. What I'm trying to find out is, what *is* it?"

Sally looked blank. "I don't understand. It's just something Uncle Willy used to have."

"I know. But how long— Do you have any idea where he got it? Or who he got it from?"

Sally shook her head, frowning. "No idea. It was just something—" She shrugged. "It was just something in that trunk, that's all."

"You don't remember him ever talking about it?"

Sally laughed. "Hardly. We didn't have that much to do with Uncle Willy, not after he got his money."

"Oh? When was that?" A faint tingle rippled across Shelbie's mind, although she couldn't say why.

"Longer ago than I really care to remember." Sally reached down and picked up the figure, turned it over in her hands. "I must've been only eight or nine at the time, so that should give you some idea."

"When you said he 'got his money,' you meant when he inherited it?" Shelbie asked, not sure why she was asking.

The older woman shook her head. "I don't know, not really. That's one of the things well-brought-up people just don't talk about, didn't you know?"

"I'd heard rumors to that effect," Shelbie said. "It's just that what you said sounded a little familiar. From what I've heard, your uncle wasn't that unlike Ben Cunningham."

"I couldn't say, actually. I'd only heard of Cunningham, never actually met him."

"Not too many people had, I understand. And no one seems to know how he got *his* money, either."

"Oh, I'm sure *somebody* must know about Uncle Willy," Sally said. "Gary, probably, but he just never talks about it. I remember I used to ask him a lot of questions, but I never got any answers, even when Willy was alive. He was sort of the black sheep—or maybe invisible sheep would be more accurate —of the family. And then he *really* ticked everyone off by killing himself."

"Yes, and I understand that it was kept pretty much of a secret," Shelbie commented.

"Very much of a secret." Sally chuckled at the distant memory. "Gary practically had apoplexy when he found out it was suicide, although I can't imagine why. He didn't know the old boy any better than the rest of us, but you'd think it was a personal insult, the way Gary carried on."

Sally looked at the figure, still in her hand, and set it back on the coffee table. "But tell me, why are you interested in this particular thing? Or in Uncle Willy at all?"

Shelbie hesitated, then decided to plunge ahead. "It's Matt— Matt Decker, the man who was here yesterday," she said, and went on to explain about Ben Cunningham's now-missing pewter figure. She even found herself talking about the odd attraction—fascination?—it seemed to hold for her, as well as the fact that some of the Cunningham estate seemed to be missing. At that point, Sally's eyebrows raised and she cocked her head sideways in a questioning look.

"Missing?" she asked when Shelbie hesitated. "You mean he didn't have as much as—Matt? Was that his name?—as much as he expected?"

"No," Shelbie said, "he had it, but he converted a lot of things into cash shortly before his death, and now no one's been able to find the cash. I don't think it's much of a secret, though. C.G.—Carson Griggs, at the *Sentinel*—knows about it; he just hasn't published anything about it yet."

Sally's expression had gone from puzzledly curious to something much stronger. She leaned forward, her eyes wide. "You mean— But of course, that's what you said, isn't it? Ben Cunningham sold what? Most of his holdings?"

Shelbie nodded. "Just about everything except the house, according to Matt."

Sally was shaking her head now, almost laughing. "And it vanished? The cash was delivered to him, and it vanished?"

Shelbie frowned. "Yes, but I don't see—"

"I don't either, but—" Sally leaned forward farther and glanced around conspiratorially as she put a hand on Shelbie's arm. "My brother would flay me alive for telling this to anyone, but this is just too good to keep! Would you believe that Uncle Willy did the same thing? Exactly the same thing!"

"What?" Shelbie tried to blink back the confusion, to think of something intelligent to say, but she couldn't.

"Uncle Willy sold everything in sight, so they told me. At tremendous losses, if you can believe Gary." She laughed again, gleeful at the memory of Gary's frustrations. "Gary was all set to have the old man— Old! He was only in his fifties! Gary was all set to have him declared incompetent, but then he killed himself before Gary had a chance. And then Gary was all set to contest the will, no matter what it turned out to be, maybe even to sue the people Willy sold his stocks and things to. But then there wasn't any will to be contested, and the money Willy had gotten had vanished, so there wasn't anything to buy the stuff back with." Sally shook her head, still chuckling at the memory. "I've never seen Gary so totally confused and frustrated— ever. All that missing money was almost worth it."

"But what happened to the money? Did you ever find out?"

"Not a trace." Sally laughed again, glancing around the room. "I've got my own theory, frankly, but . . ."

"Yes?"

Sally hesitated, a more serious note coming into her voice as she spoke. "I think Willy knew he was dying—they never performed an autopsy, you know. Gary wouldn't hear of it. I think Willy knew he was dying of something incurable, and he just didn't want Gary to get his hands on everything, so he got cash for everything and—" She stopped for a moment, a faraway look in her eyes. "I like to think maybe he gave it anonymously to some charities. Not local ones, but some in other states or even other countries. And then, before whatever it was that was killing him got too bad, he killed himself instead." She shrugged. "I like to think that, anyway."

After a long pause, Shelbie said, "And you think Ben Cunningham may have done the same thing?"

Sally looked up at Shelbie. "Makes a nice story, don't you think?"

Shelbie nodded slowly. "It makes as much sense as anything else. Except that I think there *was* an autopsy performed on Ben Cunningham."

Sally shrugged. "And Ben probably didn't dislike his nephew all that much, either."

"I don't think he knew Matt at all. Not since Matt was five or six years old, at least," Shelbie said. "But you liked *your* uncle?"

Again Sally shrugged. "I hardly knew him, either," she admitted, and then a faint smile appeared at the corners of her lips again, but there was also the suspicion of a catch in her voice as she said, "But if Gary hated him, he must've been a pretty nice guy."

CHAPTER 8

"Did you find out anything?" Matt was still several feet from Shelbie's desk in the museum as he spoke.

She looked up from the forms Cindy had finished typing before leaving for lunch a half hour before. "Nothing you couldn't have found out yourself if you'd talked to Sally instead of the others. And you? Did your search turn up anything?"

"Nothing. There's no sign of the figure. I dug through everything in the bedroom and made a quick search of the rest of the house. I could have missed it, of course, but . . . Do you think Mrs. Karns was telling the truth? You think she really did see it?"

"Why should she lie?"

"From what you said about the two of them, she might've made it up just to contradict her husband."

Shelbie shook her head. "I don't think so."

"Anyway, I couldn't find it. And Denniston claims no one else but the coroner and the sheriff have been in there, aside from people from his own office. I'll probably check with them next. But you were saying, about your talk with Sally?"

"I didn't find out anything new about the figure, but . . ." She hesitated, suddenly wondering about Sally's story. Matt had just said that Mrs. Karns might have made up something just to contradict her husband. Could Sally have been making things up—or at least exaggerating—to get even with her brother and his wife, obviously not her two favorite people?

"Yes?" Matt prompted as Shelbie remained silent.

"It looks like your uncle and Willy Brockman had more in common than money and a little pewter monster," she said, and then went on to tell him about the missing money and Sally's wistful theory.

"I don't know about Brockman," Matt said when she paused, "but the charity theory would never fit Ben Cunningham."

"You're sure? But if you didn't really know him . . ."

"From what my mother said—" He stopped, shook his head. "You could be right, I suppose. She was prejudiced—that's for sure. And a sudden burst of charity makes as much sense as his suicide. But there was no terminal illness in Uncle Ben's case. Unless the autopsy missed it . . ." His voice took on a musing quality. "I wonder if they find *everything* in an autopsy, or just the things they're looking for?"

"If any of the true crime books I've read are really true, chances are that they find only what they're looking for, especially in small town coroner's offices," Shelbie said. "You can find almost anything you want to—but only if your lab is well enough equipped *and* if you know what to look for."

"So you're saying they could've missed almost anything if they didn't suspect its existence in the first place." Matt shook his head. "No, that part of it may be possible, but not the charity . . . I wonder, though, do you suppose they knew each other?"

"Brockman and your uncle, you mean?"

"Yes. I've been thinking about the dates ever since your assistant came charging in yesterday with her news about those other suicides. It's just another coincidence, probably, but did you know that Brockman's death was just about a year before Uncle Ben suddenly turned rich?"

Shelbie blinked, feeling an uneasiness brush at her stomach. "A year? That's quite a space between them if you're hinting at a connection."

He gave a half sigh, half chuckle. "I'm not, not really. Just free-associating, I guess. That charity-suicide nonsense must've knocked loose some of my mental inhibitions." He laughed shortly. "Remember we were talking about somebody maybe blackmailing Uncle Ben? Maybe Ben was blackmailing Brockman, and that's where Ben got his sudden wealth. And he waited a year to make it look good."

Shelbie felt she should laugh, too, but something kept her from it. "You're getting really wild, Matt."

He shrugged. "I know, but why not? The sane, sensible theories don't make sense. Let's see, what haven't we covered, as long as we're going all the way? We've already hit charity and blackmail. How about if they were lovers? That gives you two reasons for the price of one, depending on how things worked out. Either love or blackmail or a combination of both. Or if that kind of love's not to your taste, how about mistresses or secret wives and families in other parts of the country? That would work for both of them as well as the other ideas. Ben certainly was away from home enough to have a secret family or two stashed away somewhere, and from what you say, so was Brockman."

Shelbie was beginning to feel uncomfortable, though she still couldn't say precisely why. "Sure," she said in an effort to treat the matter as lightly as Matt seemed to be doing, "it's simple. They were both married secretly and had a wife and family or two somewhere else under other names, and they wanted to take care of them after their deaths."

Matt was silent for a moment, and when he spoke again, most of the lightness was gone from his voice. "I get the feeling you don't think much of the idea."

"It's not that, it's just—" She stopped, shaking her head. "I don't know what it is. It's not as if it were just Brockman and your uncle. There are all those other suicides, and—"

Again she broke off, this time startled at her own words. She looked up from the desk, into Matt's face. His eyes were narrowed, a troubled frown creasing his broad forehead.

"You think there's a connection?" he asked slowly.

She shook her head vigorously, feeling her hair slap at her forehead and around her ears, and she stood up. "No, of course not. What connection could there be?"

There could be no connection, of course. It was simply coincidence, that was all, just as Sheriff Rokane had insisted—

whether he really believed it or not. Even if there *was* someone going around killing people and making it look like suicide, that would hardly account for Ben Cunningham's having converted everything into cash before being killed. No, there was no possible way there could be any connection between the missing money and the other suicides.

But why had she said it? "It's not as if it were just Brockman and your uncle." She could remember no train of thought leading up to the words. They had simply sprung, full-blown, from her mouth. She shivered, thinking once more of the irrationality of insanity, of the impossible things that would, under its influence, seem completely rational and ordinary. Acts that would seem normal, even inevitable. Theories that would seem logical, no matter how twisted and obscure. And feelings . . .

She felt pressure on her arms, and only then did she realize that Matt's hands were touching her, increasing their pressure.

"Are you all right?" he asked, just as he had asked yesterday afternoon, during another of her lapses.

"Yes, I'm fine," she said, automatically denying what she suspected was the truth.

He looked at her closely for a second, then released her. "You faded away again," he said uncertainly. "Do you always do that?"

She forced a laugh. "Not always, but often enough. Especially when something is puzzling me and I'm trying to figure it out."

"Ah," he said, taking her laugh for genuine, "a meditational trance, self-induced."

"Something like that," she agreed, and then, pulling her mind back to what she had been telling him before, pushed ahead. "Sally Marks told me something else, too."

"Yes? It sounds like you two must've hit it off famously."

"We did, but it doesn't really take all that much to get her to talk. Just a little simple curiosity, openly displayed, and an unspoken agreement that her brother is less than perfect."

"So, what else did she tell you?"

"It was an invitation, actually. To look through what's left of Brockman's house."

"What's left of it? What's that mean?"

"It was sold to a development company several years ago. They were planning another lakeside resort area, but it never came off. The company eventually went broke on another project, before they ever got started on this one. By then, though, since they'd been planning to tear everything down and start from scratch and hadn't been taking care of the place, it had deteriorated too far to be worth repairing. Vandals and curiosity seekers, mostly. But anyway, what's left of the house is still out there, if you want to take a look at it."

He hesitated. "Is there any reason we should? Other than simple curiosity?"

"Probably not," Shelbie admitted, "but isn't that reason enough?"

Some of her usual spirit seemed to be returning at the thought of exploring another old house, particularly one that had been abandoned for years. But was that all it was? Was there more than the simple tingle of curiosity and anticipation? Was that same inexplicable feeling returning once again, partially masked by her normal reaction to the thought of digging through an unfamiliar house?

She looked up at Matt and saw, for just an instant, her own puzzled mood reflected in his eyes.

"It's enough for me, certainly," he said quickly, and whatever she had seen in his eyes was gone like the mirage it had most certainly been. "Where is the place, anyway?"

"On one of the inlets on the southeast part of the lake," Shelbie said. "It's only a half mile or so from your uncle's place, as a matter of fact. With a big iron gate, too, only it's rusting away now."

"Oh, that place! I remember seeing the road running back there, but— Yes, curiosity is definitely reason enough. But unless it's changed in the last few days, there's a couple of 'No Trespassing' signs back there. Who owns it now?"

"Another development company, according to Sally. They

haven't gone broke yet, but she assured me they have no immediate plans for it and that all we have to do is go out there and trespass."

He laughed, but there was an underlying nervousness to the sound that he couldn't completely hide. "Good enough," he said. "This afternoon?"

"Why not? I don't think I'd be able to concentrate on anything else anyway, the way things have been going. And to top it all off," she added, "I think I'm starting to get nervous about my interview in Argos tonight."

"Don't worry. They'd have to be out of their minds to not take you."

"Thanks for the vote of confidence, but there must be a few people right here in Elwood who were out of their minds a couple of years ago. Otherwise I'd still be teaching." She shrugged. "But there's nothing to do about it now but wait. And looking through the Brockman place—trespassing—should be a good way of keeping my mind occupied for the afternoon. We can go as soon as Cindy gets back from lunch. All right?"

"All right." He stood silently for a moment, but then his eyes drifted toward the display case where the pewter figure was again ensconced. He looked at it, then turned back to Shelbie.

"In the meantime, I could get another errand out of the way —if I can borrow our friend for a few minutes."

Shelbie hesitated. "What now?"

"It's what I mentioned a few minutes ago—about the one that's missing from my uncle's bedroom. Maybe the sheriff or coroner saw it. I could take the thing over to the sheriff's office now, while we're waiting for Cindy to come back."

Still Shelbie hesitated. "I suppose it would be all right— although I'm beginning to think we should get some pictures taken, and then we could show those around instead of the original. The way it's been going, that thing is out of its case more than it's in."

She went to the back of the case and opened it, then stood holding the figure silently. She started to hand it to Matt, then stopped.

"Maybe *I* should show it to Lou," she said. "You two weren't on the friendliest of terms yesterday."

"That was hardly my fault. Besides, he wasn't too thrilled with you, either, when you told him about that nineteen fifty-one batch of suicides."

"I know, but still . . ." Her voice trailed off, and before she could figure out what she really wanted to say, she heard the door in the outer room clank open. A moment later, Cindy appeared in the archway. She had the remains of a Coke in one hand, a crumpled paperback in the other, and her purse was slung over one shoulder by its long strap. She looked at the two of them, then at the empty spot in the display case.

"Taking Charlie out for another walk?" she asked.

"Charlie?" Shelbie looked at her blankly.

"The little pewter critter," Cindy explained. "I had to call it *something,* and it looks a smidge like Charlie Callas with his eyes turned inside out, don't you think?"

"I hadn't noticed the resemblance," Shelbie said, looking down at the figure in her hand, "but now that you mention it . . ."

But it didn't—not really. It looked like nothing she had ever seen, and the more often she looked at it, the more she realized this. She looked up at Matt. "Do you still want to show it to Lou?"

He hesitated uncertainly, then said, "We might as well. His office isn't far."

Shelbie nodded. "Not very, just a couple of blocks. We can stop on our way out to the Brockman ruins."

He nodded but said nothing as Shelbie wrapped a tissue around the figure and dropped it once again into her purse.

Sheriff Rokane was in, but just barely. He was on his way out, but he seemed to welcome their interruption. And, except for a momentary frown of recognition, he seemed to have forgotten all about any suspicions or worries he might have had about Matt. Or about the suicide epidemics. He had probably had a long talk with his daughter last night, Shelbie thought, and her calm levelheadedness had convinced him that he had simply let his imagination run away with him temporarily. The girl had been, Shelbie remembered from when she had been in her English class, a very cool and very convincing person. Besides, the sheriff had other things on his mind.

"I have to make a speech to some women's club," he said, then looked accusingly at Shelbie. "In that same building you're in, as a matter of fact. You know them?"

"If you mean the Once-a-Weekers, yes," Shelbie said, and when he nodded, she went on sympathetically. "I'm due there in a couple of weeks myself unless I get a reprieve, and I haven't even started getting my talk together yet. I know how you feel."

"Sure you do." Rokane shook his head sadly. "If it wasn't for the election coming up in a couple of months, I'd chuck the whole thing. But what can I do for you two? If it's important enough and takes long enough, I might have an excuse to miss that meeting after all."

Shelbie laughed. "You sound pretty sneaky for a sheriff, Lou. But what we're after won't take more than a few seconds. We just want you to take a look at something."

The sheriff sighed and lowered his bulky frame onto the corner of his desk as Shelbie extracted the pewter figure from her purse. As she unwrapped it, he frowned.

"Where the devil did you get that?" he asked, reaching for it automatically.

Shelbie pulled back, suddenly gripping the figure more tightly. "What's that supposed to mean?" she asked defensively.

"That thing in your hand—what are you doing with it? How'd you get it?" He was standing over her now, frowning.

"About five minutes ago, I took it out of its display case at the museum," she said. "Now what's this all about, Lou?"

"Display case? What are you talking about? What display case?"

"If you ever came to the museum to look around, you might know."

"I'm not joking! Where did you get this?"

"I told you, Lou. It's been in a display case at the museum for—well, for at least as long as I've been working there."

"You're sure?" He was looking at the figure again, but not trying to take it from her.

"I'm sure. If you don't believe me, ask Marge. She's the one who got it in the first place."

The sheriff stood silently, his expression going from belligerence to puzzlement. "Are there more than one of those things? Is it part of a set?"

Shelbie blinked, feeling a momentary resurgence of the chill within her. "A set? Why would you think anything like that?"

"I ask the questions, Shelbie. Now, do you know of any more of these things?"

"One, at least," she admitted. "In fact, that's why we're here. Ben Cunningham had one, and the appraisers—one of them, at least—said she'd seen it in his bedroom when they were inventorying the estate. But now it's missing. Is *that* the one you're carrying on about? The one in Ben Cunningham's house?"

Rokane was silent for a long moment before he held his hand out. "Could I see it? I'll give it back."

Shelbie hesitated, then handed it to him. He turned it over slowly, looking at it from all angles. He nodded then, and handed it back to Shelbie.

"Well?" she asked. "Are you going to let us in on your secret?"

"All right," he said after another long hesitation. "I suppose the one I saw *could* have been the one Cunningham had." His voice was musing, reluctantly speculative, and he glanced toward Matt, who had been standing to one side during the entire exchange, listening but saying nothing. "I suppose," Rokane went on, "she might have taken a liking to it if she saw it, but . . ."

"Who?" Shelbie asked impatiently. "Who might have taken a liking to it?"

"Carla Schaeffer," he said slowly, looking again at the figure in Shelbie's hand. "There was one just like it in the drawer of the table next to her bed when she died."

CHAPTER 9

To no one's surprise, the sheriff ended up missing his speech to the Once-a-Weekers. Instead, he drove Shelbie and Matt out to Carla's cottage. The glass in the back door had been temporarily replaced by a piece of plywood, but the shattered glass and the flowerpot Matt had used to break it still lay on the porch floor. Rokane unlocked the door and led the way into the bedroom.

The pewter figure—Carla's pewter figure—was still in the drawer. Comparing the two figures side by side, Shelbie could see that there were differences. Slightly deeper indentations for the eyes in Carla's, for instance. Broader nose on Shelbie's, slightly fuller lips on Carla's. A scratch on Carla's but not on Shelbie's.

Not identical twins, but fraternal . . .

As he returned them to his office, the sheriff apologized for his initial suspicions. His first thought had been that Shelbie or someone had gotten into the cottage and had been playing amateur detective. "Someone like your friend Marge Remington, for instance. After you said you had told her about the so-called epidemic . . . You've got to admit that's the kind of thing she might try."

Shelbie had to agree. "But one thing you never did tell us, Lou," she said. *"Did* you see a figure like this at the Cunningham house?"

He shook his head. "No. But if I had, I would've had a few more questions for *you,* Decker, when I found this one in Miss Schaeffer's table."

Shelbie frowned puzzledly, ignoring the glance toward Matt.

"But if the figure was there only a day or two after Cunningham died, when Karns and his wife were taking inventory—"

"It may well have been," Rokane said. "The only time I was there was several days after he died. I was out of town when he killed himself, and one of the deputies handled it. And if he saw the figure, he didn't mention it. Why should he?"

"But you'll ask him about it," Shelbie said.

The sheriff nodded. "I'll ask him. All it probably means is that Miss Schaeffer did pick it up, and the one in her table is the same one that Cunningham had."

They watched silently as the sheriff's official car disappeared in the direction of the Civic Center, where he would presumably apologize for missing his speech.

"Still feel like trying to take a look at the remnants of the Brockman house?" Matt asked. They had returned the pewter figure to its place in the display case and were standing in the outer room by the door.

Shelbie hesitated, wondering. Her instinctive reaction was to put it off. Every time she turned around the last day or so, it seemed that something new and unpleasant popped up to confront her. Carla's suicide. The other recent suicides. The epidemic a quarter of a century ago. The second pewter figure in Carla's bedroom.

And Shelbie couldn't forget the "feelings" that had been assailing her. No matter how baseless they were, no matter how foolish they made her feel, she had to admit that they were— real? Well, that they existed within her, at any rate, no matter what their source.

She looked at Matt. His face was solemn now. The spirit of adventure they had both felt at the thought of exploring the Brockman house barely more than an hour earlier was gone. Still . . .

"Do you think we'd find anything worthwhile?" she asked, knowing the question was pointless.

He shrugged. "You know I don't have the faintest idea.

You're the one who brought the subject up in the first place. What do you think?" It was as if they were both trying to talk themselves out of going, but neither wanted to take the responsibility.

Shelbie shook her head. "I doubt that we'd find anything, but . . ."

"But what?" he asked when she hesitated.

"It's getting to the point where I'm almost afraid to look behind me, let alone explore another house. I have the feeling that something new is always in the process of sneaking up on me."

"I know how you feel. And you're probably right—about the house, I mean. There's really no point in our going all the way out there on a whim."

Shelbie started to nod agreement and say it would be better to skip it, at least for now, but she stopped abruptly. What was the matter with her? She couldn't let a few "feelings" and some odd coincidences get her down! Give in to things as insubstantial as that, and the next thing she knew she'd be passing out from the vapors or something else equally old-fashioned and inconsequential. And giving up like that—which was exactly what it would be, she told herself—was no way to get herself in the proper frame of mind for her interview tonight in Argos.

"Let's go take a look," she said.

"But I thought you—"

"I did, for a second, but I changed my mind. All right?" Without waiting for a reply, she pushed open the door and hurried across the alley toward the Checker. Matt looked at her retreating back for a moment and then followed.

After the first few yards, the gravel road leading back to the Brockman house was completely overgrown with grass and weeds. They were shorter in the road itself than in the ditches along each side, but that was the only distinction between road and ditch. It was more the shadow of a road than a road, and the iron gate that blocked it at the far end, in sight of the house itself, was like the rusty skeleton of a huge pair of hands. The bones sagged on their hinges, and the chain that had once held the two hands together dangled loosely to the ground, long since cut and useless.

What was left of the hinges screeched like chalk on a giant blackboard as Matt forced the gate far enough open to let them step through.

"Been a long time since anyone's been here," he said as they picked their way through the narrow opening.

Shelbie only nodded as she looked around. The house, still fifty yards distant, was partially obscured by the trees, but the outline was clearly visible. Even though the house was wood frame rather than brick and masonry, there seemed to be a vague resemblance to the Cunningham house, Shelbie thought, although it might be that she was simply looking for a resemblance. She was glad, at least, that it was midafternoon and broad daylight this time.

They walked slowly toward the house. Shelbie was glad she was wearing her usual practical outfit of jeans and flats. The weeds, including occasional burrs and thistles, would have been murder on stockings or unprotected legs, and the rough, uneven ground, effectively invisible beneath the undergrowth, would have been totally impossible for high heels. As it was, she stumbled only once in a concealed hole and recovered her balance easily.

They were standing at the bottom of what had once been a broad, stately set of steps leading up to the front door. Now the wooden steps were half-rotted and sagging, and the last coat of paint, more than a quarter of a century old, had long since peeled away. The door, broad and rounded at the top, stood ajar. All but one of the dozen windows spattered about the front of the house were broken, jagged pieces of glass still stabbing into the openings here and there.

"Well, now that we're here . . ." Matt's voice trailed away as he surveyed the remnants of the building.

Yes, Shelbie thought, now that we're here . . . "I know," she said. "Now that we're here, what are we looking for?"

"And will we recognize it if we find it?"

"Not from out here, certainly," Shelbie said abruptly. Stepping carefully but quickly, she moved up the steps and eased the door farther open. It made the same kind of noise the gate had, only lower-pitched.

"Inner Sanctum, here we come," Matt commented as he joined her in stepping through the door.

They stood facing into a long hallway which ran the length of the house. A broad staircase on the left angled grandly upward to the second floor, although much of the effect was lost because of the scattering of plaster that had fallen from the walls and ceilings and lay over everything like an uneven layer of dusty, jagged rocks. A kind of sadness spread over Shelbie as she saw that, here and there, the framework of the walls showed through the breaks in the plaster. It had taken more than simple abandonment, even for a quarter of a century, to do this. The broken windows, the plaster, the half dozen once-decorative posts torn from the stairway bannister, the pieces of chandelier scattered about the floor . . .

Then, as her eyes became more accustomed to the interior dimness, the sadness switched abruptly to irritation as she saw the more direct evidence of mindless vandalism—the crumpled, indestructible beer cans, the cellophane-wrapped remnants of cigarette packs, the butts themselves, even the petrified remains of a hot dog bun and an almost-empty potato chip sack.

"Something wrong?" Matt's voice cut into the darkness of her thoughts, and she felt his hand lightly on her shoulder.

"No, not really," she said. Then she waved her hands at the shambles around them. "It just makes me so mad every time I see something like this!" She stopped, shaking her head vigorously, as if trying to physically expel the irritation from her mind. "Come on, let's take a look around."

The ground floor had six rooms. Except for a kitchen, it was difficult to tell what any of them had been, though there were the remains of large fireplaces in two of the rooms, and one room was lined with bookshelves. The basement, unlike the Cunningham house's basement, was simply a basement, com-

plete with a furnace and now-empty storeroom. After looking
more closely at the condition of the stairs to the second floor,
they almost decided not to chance it, but finally, cautiously,
they ascended.

As on the first floor, it was difficult to guess the purpose of
the rooms, barren as they were of furniture and wall coverings.
One, with a huge fireplace and the shell of a huge picture window facing the lake, was probably the master bedroom. Or a
sitting room of some kind. The view through the huge window
was certainly the best she had seen from anywhere around the
lake. The house itself was on a small hill, and it seemed that
the trees had been deliberately arranged to frame portions of
the lake and the opposite shore and to blot out other, less
pleasing parts. The sagging piers along the eastern shore were
invisible behind a weeping willow and a cottonwood, while the
commercially developed area directly across on the north shore
was hidden by a couple of oaks. The island in the center of the
lake, though, was clearly visible, as was the totally undeveloped
swampy area along the western shore south of the line of cottages that ended with Carla's. And just south of the border of
the swamp, set back a hundred yards or so from the shore, half
hidden by the trees around it, was the Mound. She had never
seen it from this angle or this distance before, and it seemed far
more spectacular from here than it did when she was standing
next to it or climbing on it. From that close, it was simply a
small hill, rising sharply out of the trees, but from here, nearly
a mile away, it contrasted more sharply with the flatness of
wooded area around it. From here, the entire slope-sided rec-
tangular shape was visible, and Shelbie noticed for the first time
that it looked like a miniature version—a model, almost—of
the mammoth Cahokia Mound in southwestern Illinois. From
here—

From behind Shelbie came a sudden scraping sound, and she
spun around, the view through the window thrust out of her
mind. Matt was across the room, bracing himself, his hands
grasping the warped panels of a sliding door set in the far wall,
opposite the window. He had it a few inches open and was

grunting as he forced it farther back. A closet? Most likely, if this was really the master bedroom.

But then, with another grinding, scraping noise, the door flew all the way open. Matt's body blocked most of the shadowed interior of the room beyond the door as he stood silently. Then, slowly, he turned back to Shelbie.

"I'm not sure," he said, "but I think maybe we've found whatever it was we weren't expecting to find and wouldn't recognize if we did find it."

His voice, though casual on the surface, held a tension that only accentuated the chill that had suddenly spread across Shelbie's back. "What is it?" she asked, beginning to pick her way across the plaster-littered floor toward him.

"Like I said, I'm not sure." He stepped to one side as she reached him. "Here, you take a look."

She hesitated then, but only for a moment, frowning up at him as she reached the door. At first, as her eyes adjusted to the shadows, she saw only another littered floor and more peeling, disintegrating walls. A closet, that was all, so why was Matt—

But it wasn't a closet, she suddenly realized. It was a room— a tiny, windowless room, behind what had once been a sliding door. A tiny room, just large enough for a single chair to have been placed in its center.

A tiny room, totally bare except for the single arch-topped niche—altar?—that was sunken into one wall . . .

CHAPTER 10

The afternoon had turned cloudy and unseasonably cold while they had been inside the remnants of the Brockman mansion. As they pushed their way back through the knee-high grass and weeds toward the waiting Checker, Shelbie felt the dry north wind buffeting her back, biting through the light sweater she wore. Behind them, she thought she could hear it whistling through the shell of the house, but she knew that, more likely, it was simply the sound it made as it swept through the trees and past her own ears.

Finally, they were past the sagging iron gate and inside the car. For a long moment, they sat silently, watching the clouds as they thickened and spread across the sky, blotting out the last traces of blue. As a gust of wind, seeming to come directly from the house itself, rocked the car ever so slightly on its springs, Matt started the engine and began backing cautiously down the long, narrow drive to the road.

As they bumped backward across the entrance to the drive and into the road, Shelbie realized that she had been holding her breath for several seconds. She let it out in a whoosh and shook her head sharply.

"What does it mean, Matt?"

"The little room?" When she said nothing, he went on. "I haven't the faintest idea. What about you?"

"I don't know. But it's got to mean *something!*"

"They're both old houses," he said. "Maybe it was some sort of fad that was making the rounds in the late eighteen-hundreds or whenever they were built."

"Fad? But what are the rooms for?"

"You're the one who runs the historical society," he said. "Weren't there lots of odd little rooms they used to build into houses? Pantries? Maids' rooms?"

"Some, but nothing like those two rooms. Tell me the truth; have you ever seen anything like them?"

He shook his head, not taking his eyes from the road. "A little dressing room, maybe? They were next to bedrooms. My uncle's was, at least."

"Not likely," she said, and Matt didn't disagree. After a time, she went on. "I'll ask Marge sometime. She dug through more old houses than I ever did. Maybe she'll have an idea."

Somehow, the simple fact of their words, whether anything was resolved or not, was already beginning to peel away some of the mystery. The rooms were, after all, just that—rooms. And the fact that there was one in the Brockman house as well as the Cunningham house was just a coincidence. Or, as Matt had suggested, the rooms were something that had been commonplace when the houses had been built in the nineteenth century.

Matt glanced at his watch. "It's getting late. What time did you say your interview was in Argos?"

Hastily, she looked at her own watch. "I still have a couple of hours," she said. "I don't have to be there until seven, but . . ." She looked down at her jeans and sweater. "But I do have to get ready. They're not going to hire an English teacher in grubby jeans—that's for sure."

Matt was silent for a moment as they slowed for an unmarked, intersecting road. "I can drop you off at your car at the museum," he said as they accelerated along the curving road, the lake occasionally visible through the trees on the left, "or I could drop you off at your apartment and then drive you up to Argos for your interview. If you want the company."

"There's no need, Matt," she said quickly. "It's almost twenty miles, and you'd just have to cool your heels in the hall while I'm in there getting the third degree."

He shrugged. "If you don't want me to . . ."

"It's not that. It's just that it would be a lot of trouble and wasted time for you, that's all."

"Depends on how you look at it," he said. "I don't have anything important to do tonight. And when you're through, we can stop somewhere and celebrate your new job. There used to be a pretty good pizza parlor at the edge of Argos."

She laughed. "It's still there, the last I looked."

He looked at her for a moment. "Well? How about it?"

"All right," she said, "but drop me off at my car anyway. I'll drive it home, and you can pick me up in an hour. All right?"

He nodded and glanced at his watch again, but said nothing. After a few seconds, Shelbie settled back in the seat herself, feeling more than slightly relieved that Matt would be going with her. There was something about him, something solid—solid and unchanging. Which was, after her years with C.G., something to be desired. Although C.G. probably hadn't really changed that much, she thought. He had always been the same way, but he had kept it hidden at first. . . .

Cindy was gone and the museum locked when Matt left her in the parking lot next to her car, but there was a note stuck under the windshield wiper.

"C.G. stopped by to wish you luck with your job and to take another look at Charlie," the note said in Cindy's characteristic scrawl. "And call me as soon as you can for another surprise." Shelbie ignored Matt's questioning look and crumpled the paper and tossed it into the litter bag she kept suspended from the unused cigarette-lighter knob on the dash. The last thing she needed tonight was another surprise, particularly if it had anything to do with C.G.

The interview went badly from the minute it was revealed that not only was Shelbie divorced, but she had resumed her "maiden name." Oddly enough, though, the only member of the Argos school board who seemed to object was the youngest member, Bert Harris, probably no older than Shelbie herself, dressed in modern—though not mod—clothes, his hair fashionably long and casual. His opposition was apparently enough, and his slyly antagonistic questions were enough to badger Shelbie into returning the fire once or twice, and that, in turn, was enough to make the other members at least neutral toward her and unwilling to stand up against Harris.

As she emerged into the empty, echoing hallway after the ordeal was finished, Matt recognized the expression on her face immediately.

"Bad?" he asked.

"Not good. How do you feel about a pizza wake instead of a pizza celebration?"

"That bad? What happened?"

She shrugged as they walked down the hall toward the outer door, their footsteps echoing hollowly from the cold plaster walls.

"One of them had it in for divorcées, or that's the way it sounded. And I let my temper show a couple of times."

"Divorcées? You're kidding! In this day and age?"

"In this day and age, yes. Believe me, you still run into a few like that, particularly on school boards." She was silent a moment, her mind wandering back to the year before. "In fact," she went on with another shrug, "I wouldn't be totally astonished to learn that my divorce had a little something to do with my losing my job in Elwood."

Matt held the door open for her and followed her down the steps toward the parking lot. "I thought that sort of thing went out with the Middle Ages. Besides, isn't discrimination like that supposed to be illegal now? Wasn't there something you could do about it?"

"Lots of things are illegal," she said, a trace of bitterness in her voice, "but they happen anyway. And maybe I could've done something about it, if I'd had proof. I could've filed suit, but it would've cost money and gotten me nowhere for at least a year. And earned me more enemies than I already had."

Matt unlocked the Checker door and held it open for her. "You really think you lost the job because of the divorce?" he asked as he climbed in behind the wheel.

"Who knows? I have no proof, if that's what you mean. The

coincidence is hard to ignore, that's all. Divorced in early spring, out of a job in the fall. Notified too late to look for anything else, unfortunately."

"The school board in Elwood is conservative? Or what?"

"As I may have said before, who knows? No more conservative than a lot of small-town school boards, but a couple of them were just like Harris was tonight."

"Harris?" He glanced toward Shelbie as the car paused at the exit from the school parking lot.

"He's the one who had it in for me just now." She smiled faintly as she shook her head. "He seemed to take the whole thing personally. You'd think I divorced him instead of C.G. Unless I'm just being paranoid."

"I doubt that." He was silent as they moved through the Argos business district: a couple of dozen stores, all closed in the evening, and a movie theater. "So you're still out of a paying job, then. No other prospects?"

"Not at the moment, and it's getting late again. Schools start in a couple of weeks, and they've been mostly filled up since midsummer. I may still get in a little substitute teaching around the county, but that's probably all. It looks like another year with good old FCHS."

"FCHS?"

"Farrell County Historical Society. I can probably survive, but . . . To tell the truth, though, one of these days I'm going to forget my principles and take Dad up on his offer. Or did I tell you about that?"

"Not that I remember. Your father used to be a teacher here in Elwood, didn't he?"

She nodded. "Until five or six years ago. He's principal up at Perrysburgh now. Last year he offered to pull a few strings for me up there."

Matt was silent again for two or three blocks, and then the lights of the restaurant—pizza parlor—blinked into existence ahead and to the right.

"Have you ever thought about a larger city?" Matt asked, keeping his eyes on the street ahead of them.

Shelbie glanced toward him. "Depends on the city and the school. Why?"

"There *might* be an opening or two later on this year in Claymore."

"That's where you're living now?"

He nodded, still concentrating on driving, or so it seemed from the way he kept his eyes straight ahead.

"It's what—fifty thousand?" she asked.

"More like seventy-five. And they're just getting into the integration business, a step ahead of a court order, and I suspect a few of the old-timers will be leaving. Retiring early or just quitting."

"They're expecting trouble?"

"There're always a few who expect—and find—trouble everywhere they look. And if they can't find it, they stir it up themselves. Anyway, whatever the reasons, there may be an opening or two later this year, if you'd care to put your name in."

For a moment, she thought of everyone she knew in Elwood; but for another moment, she considered her financial state and the ever-present C.G. waiting in the wings.

"Why not?" she said as Matt turned into the restaurant parking lot. "How soon do I have to get my application in?"

Matt seemed to relax with her words. "I'll give Jack Avery a call in the morning, just to see how things are going. He's on the school board, and he works in my office. A draftsman—or illustrator, rather. I'll let you know what he says, though there probably isn't any great rush to put in a formal application."

"And Jack Avery isn't prejudiced against divorced women?" Her tone was light, but there was a touch of seriousness that wasn't completely hidden.

Matt grinned as the car rolled to a stop and he reached past Shelbie to unlatch the door on her side of the car. "He even gets along with his *own* ex-wife," he said, "who just happens to be a teacher, too. Although she didn't go so far as to take her maiden name back after the divorce. But there are rumors floating around that they may be getting back together one of these days."

Shelbie shrugged as she climbed out of the car. "There are rumors like that about C.G. and me, too, but they were all started by C.G."

"I get the feeling that Mr. Griggs doesn't give up easily."

Shelbie laughed, a not-altogether-amused sound, as Matt locked the Checker and they moved toward the restaurant. "You could say that, I suppose," she said. "If you want to try your luck in the 'biggest understatement of the year' sweepstakes. But that's enough about C.G. and rumors for one night. All right?"

"Agreed," he said, holding the door for her.

Somehow, they did manage to avoid not only C.G. and divorce but school boards as well until they were almost back to Elwood. For one thing, it wasn't long before Shelbie, in answer to a fairly simple question, got started on the foibles of the historical society.

"What it really takes to run one," she said at one point, "is a horse trader. Or maybe con artist or compromiser would be closer to the truth. At least that's the way it seems to work for these small, largely unfunded societies. And Marge was one of the best. There were only forty or fifty members when she took over, and by the time she left, there were almost five hundred. And the museum in the Civic Center—that's her doing, too, in a way. At least she talked the city council into renting her the quarters for practically nothing. Although the fact that all that term's councilmen are life members of the society, free, might have something to do with it. Not to mention that a couple of the key councilmen are written up in *Farrell County Folks*."

Matt frowned thoughtfully for a second. "Wasn't that one of those books I saw on the museum sale shelf?"

"That's right. And we're going to do another volume one of these days, provided we ever get it finished and sent off to the printer. Which reminds me, that's something else I should be doing instead of checking out abandoned houses and ugly little statues."

"Is there anything I can do to help?" Matt asked. "It only seems fair, since you've been using your time to help me with my wild hunches."

She thought for a moment. "You did say you were a technical writer, didn't you?"

"That's right. Why?"

"So you know a little grammar and punctuation, and you'd recognize a complete sentence if you saw one?"

He chuckled and shook his head. "I do and I would, but that has nothing to do with the fact that I'm a tech writer."

"How would you feel about some nontechnical writing? Specifically, a dozen or so manuscripts from some of the people we're including in the second volume. They need 'cleaning up,' some more than others. Interested?"

"Why not? As I said, I owe you a few hours, certainly. Where are they? At the museum?"

"My apartment, I think. I haven't looked at them for a couple of weeks, but the last I remember, that's where they were. You want to pick them up tonight?"

"Is that an invitation?"

Abruptly, much of the lightness evaporated from her mood, and she looked toward Matt. His eyes were still on the road, his expression relaxed. After a moment of silence, he glanced at her questioningly.

"I guess it is," she said, "if you want to stop by for a few minutes."

A slight frown lowered his brows a fraction. "Did I say something I shouldn't have?" he asked.

She shook her head, embarrassed that he had spotted the change in her attitude so easily. "No, it's not you. It's me—I think. I'm afraid I've been a little too defensive lately, ever since I split up with C.G."

"Oh? Because of your troubles with him? Or something else?" The question was simple, matter-of-fact, like Matt himself, and Shelbie suddenly realized that she did feel—feel *something* for Matt. But what? It was certainly not anything like the postrescue syndrome of admiration and gratitude that had driven her so precipitately into C.G.'s arms. And Matt was hardly what you would call excessively handsome—just sort of passable, neither handsome nor homely. And what with his preoccupation with following his "hunches" about the pewter figure and his late uncle, he could hardly be said to have swept her off her feet.

And yet . . .

Finally, Shelbie recognized the feeling, and she wondered why it had taken so long. It was so simple. The way she felt, purely and simply, was *comfortable*. With C.G., except for a few days of postpanic euphoria, there had always been a tension, a holding back for fear of leaving herself open to his disapproval. Never had either of them completely relaxed with the other. And with other men since the divorce, matters had been no better. But now, after only two days, for no discernible reason, she felt completely at home with Matt Decker.

She shook her head bemusedly, wondering at her own thoughts and reactions. She looked at Matt, whose eyes were alternating between her and the red light they had stopped at.

"Sorry," he said, "I didn't mean to be nosy."

"That's all right," she said. "You weren't. I was just thinking about something, that's all."

"And the results?"

"Nothing spectacular. Just getting some thoughts sorted out. But you were asking why I had been getting on the defensive."

"You don't have to—"

"That's all right. I'd just as soon talk about it. To tell the truth, it'll probably do me some good. Just thinking about it seems to have helped already." She laughed and leaned back in the seat. "You know, Mr. Decker, has anyone ever told you that you're something of an old shoe?"

"Not in so many words. Is that good or bad?"

"Good. For me, at least. I get the feeling I can relax around you. And when you're divorced, and you live in a small town, that is not a feeling you get very often."

A few minutes later, the Checker rolled to a stop at the curb in front of Shelbie's apartment. Matt took her arm lightly as they started up the outside stairs. Halfway up, Shelbie stiffened, listening.

"The phone!" she said hastily and dashed up the rest of the steps, fumbling her purse open as she went. It rang three more times before she managed to get the key out and unlock the door, and another two while she pushed the door open and dashed across the room.

"Hello?"

"Shelbie? Is that you? You sound funny."

"Just out of breath from running up the stairs. Cindy?"

"That's right. Didn't you find my note under your windshield wiper?"

"I found it, but— This was my night for Argos, remember? That was part of your note, in case you forgot."

"Argos? Oh yes, the job. How did it go?"

"It didn't."

"I'm sorry," Cindy said, but her voice didn't sound particularly sorrowful. "But wait till you hear what *we* found today!"

"We?"

"Marge Remington and Tim and me. She came by this afternoon, to see if you'd come up with anything new, and—"

"And you told her about that other suicide epidemic in nineteen fifty-one."

"That's right. And then we all got to talking about it, about how strange it all was, and—" Cindy paused to take in a breath. "And you'll never guess what we found then!"

"Found where?" Shelbie wasn't sure what they were leading up to, but she was already feeling a faint chill working its way along her spine.

"In the old *Sentinel* files at the library," Cindy said animatedly. "Actually, Tim's the one who found it—he and his mother. I had to stick around the museum till it closed, but— But what they found is *another* epidemic, this time in *nineteen twenty-six!*"

CHAPTER 11

The chill was suddenly full grown, covering Shelbie's entire back like an icy blanket. "You're sure? You couldn't be—"

"I'm sure, Shelbie! There were five in a three-month period! All but one was in his or her early twenties, just like the other two times!" Despite the excitement in Cindy's voice, there was something else, something that reminded Shelbie of the chill that was clutching at her own back.

"Did you tell the sheriff?" Shelbie asked.

Cindy laughed nervously. "What for? You know how he reacted when you told him about the others, the ones in nineteen fifty-one. And these are *really* ancient history! Besides, he'll find out in a day or so. In fact, everyone will. Marge is putting out a special edition of the *Bugle*. With any kind of luck—and a little credit—she can get it printed tomorrow."

"Is that where you are now? At Marge's?"

"Right. I'm proofreading. And I've been trying to get hold of you most of the evening. I'd forgotten all about your job interview, the way things have been going. But now that you're back, would you like to look over what we've done so far? See if you have anything to add? Or correct?"

Shelbie hesitated, glancing toward Matt, who was standing by the door, watching her curiously.

"After all," Cindy's voice came over the line, "you did start this whole thing, in a way, with that suicide epidemic talk yesterday morning. You and that Matt Decker. Incidentally, have you seen him this evening? I tried his motel a couple of times, but no luck. And since his uncle was part of the current batch—"

"He's right here," Shelbie interrupted. "He drove me up to Argos and back."

Matt moved across the room toward her. "Someone want me?" he asked, looking at the phone in her hand.

Shelbie shook her head, covered the mouthpiece with one hand. "It's Cindy. She and Marge came up with another . . . epidemic." Her own voice sounded strangely subdued to her, and the chill strengthened its hold on her until it was almost a physical pressure against her spine. "Marge is—"

"*Another?* When?" The words were uncharacteristically sharp for Matt.

"Nineteen twenty-six," Shelbie said.

Matt blinked. "Nineteen twenty-six . . . That's twenty-five years before those others, and they were twenty-four years before the ones this year. . . ." He reached out for the phone. "Let me talk to her a second, all right?"

Shelbie handed him the receiver.

"Cindy? This is Matt Decker. Shelbie says you came across another batch of suicides today, from nineteen twenty-six."

"Matt? What happened to Shelbie? I was talking to her, and—"

"It's all right. She's right here. I just want to ask you a couple of things."

"Sure, but—"

"Those new suicides you found—were they all young? Or were they like the other two batches? All young but one?"

There was a brief silence, and when Cindy spoke again, her voice was subdued. "They were all in their early or mid-twenties, except for the first. She was fifty-three."

Matt glanced toward Shelbie before speaking into the phone again. "A woman this time?"

"Rebecca Emrick."

"Did you check any further back?" Matt asked slowly.

"At least a year. There was just one—"

"No, I mean another twenty-four or -five years, or maybe more. Around nineteen-hundred, say."

Another pause. "No, but we *were* thinking about it. In the

morning, we can—" Cindy stopped abruptly, then resumed, speaking rapidly. "Look, can you and Shelbie come over here this evening? If you want the truth, this whole thing is beginning to scare the daylights out of me!"

He was silent a moment, glancing toward Shelbie again. "All right," he said, "we'll be over in a few minutes." Without waiting for a reply, he hung up.

"You heard?" he asked Shelbie.

"I heard enough. The nineteen twenty-six batch was the same as the other two, right? One middle-aged and rich, followed by a half dozen or so in their twenties?"

Matt nodded. "Middle-aged, anyway. Cindy didn't say if she was rich or not."

"She? A woman this time?"

"Rebecca Emrick, she said. The name mean anything to you?"

For the moment it took Shelbie to start to shake her head, the name didn't register. But then it did.

Rebecca Emrick . . .

"I'm not a hundred percent sure," Shelbie said slowly, "but I *think* she once owned the house your uncle lived in."

"Which means she was very definitely rich," he said softly. "I just hope it doesn't turn out that *her* money disappeared, too. Or that there really *was* another batch of suicides around nineteen-hundred."

Shelbie couldn't repress a shudder. "You said something about going over to Marge's tonight. Did Cindy ask you to help out on the *Bugle,* too?"

Matt shook his head. "She's just getting scared, and I can't say that I blame her."

"Scared? Cindy? She didn't sound scared a couple of minutes ago, just enthusiastic."

"The same way she did yesterday for a while? Before it all started sinking in? There's an expression that covers the situation—whistling past the graveyard, or something like that."

Shelbie started to protest, but she stopped before she could get a word out. Matt was right, of course. Cindy had cooled off considerably yesterday as the reality of the situation worked its way into her mind. And today, after finding yet another rash of suicides, these nearly a half century old . . .

That was a pretty big graveyard, and you had to do a lot of whistling and shouting to keep up your courage as you tried to race past it, especially if, each time you thought you were safely past, you saw another row of tombstones stretching on ahead of you. Cindy was just lucky that she was in the company of one of the best graveyard whistlers in the business—Marge Remington. Some of Marge's expertise in the area must have rubbed off on Cindy.

Maybe, Shelbie thought, she could use a little of it herself. So far, things had been happening so fast that she hadn't taken the time to think things through, not completely. So far, it had simply been a series of events and discoveries, and, while she had speculated on possible causes, she had never really, seriously tried to tie them all together.

At first, when it had been only Carla's suicide and Shelbie's own "feelings," she had thought of insanity as an explanation more than once. But it was obvious now that it was more than that. Insanity, no matter how bizarre its form, could account for only so much. It could not account for three separate rashes of suicide over a period of a half century. And, on the more pedestrian side, it certainly could not account for the money that had disappeared not once but twice.

No, whatever had happened—whatever *was* happening—the implication was both plain and terrifying. Someone—or some *thing,* a corner of her mind told her chillingly—was making it happen.

Abruptly, the darkness beyond the curtained windows of her apartment seemed cold and frightening, not for what it was but for what she now knew it must contain. Somewhere out there—

The sudden jangle of the phone snatched her from her deep and unwelcome reverie so sharply that she came within a fraction of screaming. By the time she had crossed the room and picked up the receiver, though, she had pulled in a deep breath and forced herself into at least a semblance of calmness.

"Hello. Cindy?"

"Ms. Wilson? Shelbie Wilson?" The voice, a woman's, was hesitant, nervous.

"That's right. Who is this?"

"My name is Harriet Nordstrom. I was—"

"I remember you, Mrs. Nordstrom," Shelbie said, frowning as she cut the other woman off. Shelbie could see the woman's rounded face and uncertain expression in her mind's eye as her thoughts darted involuntarily back to the Argos school board meeting. "What can I do for you?"

"I—I just wanted you to know that Mr. Harris did not speak for—for all of us," the woman said, slowly and hesitatingly.

"Thank you," Shelbie said coldly. For the moment, fantasy thoughts of suicide epidemics and things in the night were forced out of her mind.

Mrs. Nordstrom swallowed audibly. "Personally, I would have—" she began, then stopped, and Shelbie could hear the woman's breath coming out in an uneven sigh.

"But I didn't, did I?" Mrs. Nordstrom went on a moment later, her voice quiet and uninflected. With the admission, much of the tension seemed to drain out of her, replaced by a certain sadness. "I didn't do a thing . . ."

Abruptly, the woman was no longer an enemy, Shelbie realized. If she had ever been an enemy at all. A twinge of guilt hovered over Shelbie for an irrational moment, and her face softened.

"Is there something I can do for you?" Shelbie asked, and this time her voice was open and inviting.

There was a brief silence as the other woman seemed to become aware of the change in tone. Then she said, "Thank you. I wouldn't blame you if you refused to even speak to me. If anyone should have stood up for you, I should have. But I didn't, more's the shame."

"It's all right," Shelbie said, then grinned ruefully. "Actually, it's not, but there's nothing that can be done about it now, and there's no need for us to be at each other's throats. I've survived worse than this."

"You're more than generous," Mrs. Nordstrom said, "but I really should have spoken up for you. I know how it is. I—I was divorced myself once, several years ago. I wasn't a teacher, but . . ." The woman's voice trailed off, and some of the tension seemed to return to fill the silence.

"Was there something else?" Shelbie asked finally.

Shelbie could hear the indrawn breath at the other end of the line. It was a nervously determined sound, and then Mrs. Nordstrom began to speak again, choosing her words slowly and carefully.

"I can't be positive," she said, "not completely positive, but I *think* it was a put-up job. I—"

"Put-up job?" Shelbie frowned. "I don't follow you."

"Mr. Harris and—" Mrs. Nordstrom swallowed audibly. "Mr. Harris and your ex-husband, I believe."

"C.G.? What could C.G. have to do with anything?" But even as Shelbie asked, a curiously empty feeling surged through her, and she was sure that she already knew the answer.

"As I said, I can't be completely sure, but— Your ex-husband does run the *Elwood Sentinel,* doesn't he?"

"That's right."

"Well, Mr. Harris is running for the state house of representatives from this district, and I'm reasonably sure that this district includes Elwood."

The emptiness Shelbie had felt seconds before was giving way to anger. "And your Mr. Harris has been talking to C.G. lately?" she asked.

"I—I don't know, not for sure. But for the last few days, Mr. Harris *has* been talking about the unqualified and valuable support he expects to get from the *Elwood Sentinel*. I didn't think much about it, not until tonight, when I saw how he treated you, and when I realized who you were. He—he really isn't normally that way. Two of the teachers we hired last year were divorced, and he didn't object at all. But the way he attacked you personally tonight—well, there just has to be a reason, don't you see?"

Shelbie's fingers tightened on the receiver, and the lines of her jaw hardened. It fits, she thought, the anger twisting at her stomach. It fits! He won't give up, ever! He just won't give up!

"Thank you, Mrs. Nordstrom," Shelbie said, forcing her voice to remain steady, barely resisting the impulse to slam the receiver down.

"I'm sorry," the older woman said. "I probably shouldn't have said anything to you, not without proof, but it seemed so unfair, I just couldn't— I know it's too late to do any good, but I had to let you know."

"I appreciate it, believe me," Shelbie said tightly, formally. "I know how hard it must have been for you."

"Yes. Yes, it was." The nervousness was returning to the woman's voice. "But I had to— I had to let you know. I couldn't— I'm sorry."

The line went dead, and Shelbie dropped the phone into the cradle. She barely saw Matt as she turned and started toward the door. Her stomach twisted into a knot, and all she could think was: That tears it! That really tears it! If he thinks he can get away with this . . .

At that moment, she was thinking no further ahead than the instant of confrontation, when C.G. came to the door and had to face her. There was no thought as to what she would say or do, beyond telling him that she knew what he was trying to do and that he would not get away with it. There was only the boiling anger within her that seemed to tense every muscle in her body as she walked.

At the door, she felt Matt's hand on her arm, restraining her.

"More trouble?" his voice asked, but she only shook her head and shrugged off the hand.

Outside the door, at the head of the steps, she paused briefly. "You go ahead to Marge's," she said, her voice tightly controlled. "I'll meet you there in a few minutes."

Then she was moving rapidly down the steps, only peripherally aware of the door of her apartment slamming behind Matt as he hurried after her. She dug vigorously through her purse as she moved, throwing the contents into even more of a disarray than had existed before, but she found her keys before she reached her car.

"Shelbie!" Matt grabbed at the car door as she slid behind the wheel and started to pull the door shut. "I don't know what that phone call was all about, but whatever it was, you look too upset to drive. I'll take you wherever you want to go."

Ignoring him, she jabbed the key into the ignition. A moment later the engine coughed into life, and then roared and vibrated the entire car as she jammed the accelerator almost to the floor.

"Shelbie, whatever it is—"

"I'll meet you at Marge's later!" With all her strength, Shelbie yanked inward on the door, and Matt, taken by surprise, avoided crushed fingers only by inches as he jerked his hand away.

The wheels spit gravel as she jammed the gears into reverse. The car almost bottomed out on its springs as the wheels bounced through the sudden drop at the end of the driveway. If the engine had had a few more horsepower, the tires would have squealed as she moved off down the street.

Gradually, though, control returned. There were a dozen stop lights and stop signs between Shelbie's apartment and C.G.'s house on the opposite side of town, and with each hard-braked stop and engine-racing start, a bit of her fury was transformed into rational thought. She didn't *know* that C.G. was responsible for her losing the job tonight, though it was certainly likely. And she didn't *know* that he had been responsible for her contract not being renewed here in Elwood, though if the one were true, the other probably followed. So the first thing she must do was find out for sure, one way or the other.

And chances were, if she asked C.G., he would tell her. Lying was not—at least it had not been—one of his faults. In fact, she thought as she turned onto the street where the two of them had lived for three years, he would probably admit his guilt freely.

Except—and the thought made her hands tighten convulsively on the wheel once again—except that he would or could not see it as guilt. He would regret the necessity for causing her any temporary inconvenience, but he would simply see it as one more logical step in his campaign to get her back, to protect her, to make her come to her senses and realize that being a cherished possession of Carson Griggs was a signal honor that no young woman in her right mind would ever turn down.

She shook her head violently, swearing under her breath. If there was one thing she had to do before confronting C.G., it was calm down. She had to be completely in control. To be otherwise would only make it worse; it would be playing into his hands. If she displayed the faintest hint of emotion, he would turn it back on her, pointing it out as simply one more piece of proof that she was better off with him, under his guidance.

Under his ownership was more like it!

With an effort, Shelbie forced her fingers to loosen their white-knuckled grip on the steering wheel. Calmness. Rationality. Those were the keys.

She slowed the car almost to a stop while still a good two blocks from the house. She took a deep breath, and then, for an instant, she purposely tensed and strained every muscle in her body, crushing the upheaval in her stomach. When she relaxed, she felt limp.

There were no lights on in the house as she coasted slowly to a stop by the curb, but C.G.'s Mercedes was in the carport. Which meant that he was at home, since he never let anyone else drive him anywhere, and he certainly never walked anywhere. But why were the lights out? It was barely ten o'clock.

She was walking up the steps onto the imitation Colonial front porch—which had always looked out of place on a house no larger than this one—when a car rolled to a quick stop in the street. She glanced around in time to see Matt climbing out of his Checker and starting toward her.

For a moment, some of the anger boiled up in her again, but then it was gone. No matter what else Matt was, he was a far cry from C.G. And, now that she thought about it, it might not be a bad idea for Matt to be here with her. If nothing else, his presence might have some slight effect on C.G., if only to prove to him that other men did exist, even right here in Elwood.

She waved at him as he hurried up the walkway. She even managed a smile. Apparently seeing the change in her mood, Matt hesitated on the steps below her.

"You're all right?" he asked.

"I'm better than I was, let's say." She beckoned him the rest of the way with a wave of her hand. "Come on up, Matt."

He looked at her cautiously as he came up the remaining steps. "Does this mean I've gotten my old-shoe status back?"

She blinked, then remembered her remark from a while before. "If you want it," she said.

"Why else would I have trailed you all the way across town after you came within a whisker of mashing my fingers in your car door? Now, what's this all about? Where are we?"

Quickly she explained, all the while wondering why C.G. hadn't come to the door to see what was going on. She and Matt weren't shouting, but neither were they holding their voices to a whisper; even if C.G. was sleeping, it normally didn't take much to wake him.

Matt shook his head in wonder when she had finished. "I didn't think people like that still existed any more," he said.

"Neither did I," Shelbie said, "until it was too late. As long as he was the 'struggling young editor,' my having a decently paying job fit in with his plans perfectly; but when he started running for public office, it got in the way. I was supposed to drop everything to campaign for him, just be the 'perfect wife.'"

"But he didn't fight the divorce?"

Shelbie shook her head. "He didn't want the publicity. He was afraid any kind of fight would cost him votes. And he thought—still thinks!—that if he gives me enough time, I'll come back on my own. You have no idea—"

She broke off, closing her eyes for a moment. "But if I get started on that again, you'll be in for the whole fifty-cent lecture. And there's no point in discussing C.G.'s merits by ourselves." She turned and jabbed at the doorbell. The double tone of the chimes was clearly audible through the door.

"You're sure he's here?" Matt asked, looking again at the darkened windows.

"He's here," she said. "He never goes around the block without his chariot, and in all the time I knew him, he never once rode in a car that someone else drove."

There was still no response to the bell, and Shelbie jabbed at it again, then pounded solidly on the door with her fist. "He's here, I know it! He's here!"

"Easy," Matt said, putting a hand on her arm, "or you'll have a stroke right here on the porch, and that's not easy for someone your age."

She took another deep breath. Matt was right, of course. She had gotten herself calmed down once, so there was no point in getting worked up all over again.

"Don't worry," she said, "I'm still in control, more or less. But you—"

A light came on inside the house.

"See? I told you he was home." Shelbie's voice held a note of triumph. The light, barely visible through the window to the right of the door, was coming from the hallway that led to the bedroom. Just to hurry him along, Shelbie jabbed the button one more time. Matt stood silently a couple of steps behind her.

Finally, the lights in the foyer came on, and the door opened a crack. Griggs peered through the narrow opening. His black hair was in an uncharacteristic tangle, and his normally sharp eyes seemed heavy with the remnants of sleep. His robe, usually as neat and formal appearing as most people's evening clothes, was fastened loosely around the waist.

For a moment, Shelbie was silent, puzzled by his appearance. He had always prided himself on—among other things—his ability to be totally alert the instant he woke up. Was he sick? Was that why—

Sharply, irritably, Shelbie cut off that line of thought. The state of his health had nothing to do with why she was here.

"I just got back from Argos," she said without preamble. "I met a friend of yours, a Mr. Harris."

Griggs looked at her blankly, as if he wasn't completely sure who she was. Then he blinked, and his body straightened itself with an effort. It was as if he were struggling to come out of a daze.

"Shelbie? What are you doing here?" His voice, too, seemed uncharacteristically uncertain.

"I just told you, C.G. I met a friend of yours in Argos, a Mr. Harris. You do know Bert Harris, don't you?"

"Harris? I'm not— Oh, yes, Harris." He blinked again, shook his head, and ran his outsized hand through his hair. "What about him?"

"That's what I was about to ask you, C.G. What *about* Mr. Harris? *Did* you offer to give him *Sentinel* support if he would make sure I didn't get the job?"

Finally, Griggs seemed to be coming fully awake. He blinked once more, straightened his shoulders, and attempted to smooth out the robe. This was more like the C.G. she knew, Shelbie thought as a faintly amused smile appeared on his face. He stood back and opened the door more widely.

"Won't you come in, Shelbie? And Mr.—Mr. Decker, isn't it?"

"No, thank you," Shelbie said, relieved in a way to see at least the partial return of the real Carson Griggs. "All I want is an answer to my question."

"Your question? Oh yes, about Harris." His smile broadened, and his face was now saturated with self-assurance—even more than was usual for him, Shelbie thought. "What was it you wanted to know about him, Shel? And you're positive you won't step inside? Even with your chaperon?"

"Just answer the question, C.G. That's all I want from you tonight." She could feel the familiar tightness in her stomach, and she was beginning to doubt her wisdom in coming here at all. It had been nothing more than an impulse, and she had known from the start that nothing worthwhile could be accomplished.

He shrugged lightly. "Very well. Now, the question. What was it again? Something about Bert Harris, wasn't it?"

"You know what the question was! Did you or did you not make sure that he wouldn't let me get that job tonight?"

"Oh yes, that. You didn't really want to teach there, did you? From what I've heard, it's really a quite unpleasant school."

"Did you or didn't you, C.G.? Yes or no!"

Another shrug. "Very well. Yes. And if you—"

"And when my contract wasn't renewed last year? Did you have a hand in that, too?"

The faint smile, more impossibly self-satisfied than ever, broadened slightly. There was not even the trace of regret she had expected him to show for the "temporary" pain he was causing her. "A hand? In a manner of speaking, I did. In a few days, however, you will see—"

"Why? For God's sake, why? Can't you get it through your head that it's over? It's *been* over for the last year and a half, and every harebrained stunt like this that you pull—"

She stopped abruptly as she felt Matt's hand on her arm. She realized she had been almost shouting, which was just what she had told herself she would not do.

"All right, C.G.," she said, her voice low and even now, "you do whatever you want. But you can't get your hooks into someone on every school board in the state!"

Abruptly, she turned, brushing against Matt's arm, and walked briskly off the porch and down the steps, Matt following closely behind her. At the car, she glanced back at the door, only to see Griggs still standing there, the same confident smile plainly visible even at that distance.

CHAPTER 12

Shelbie was still steaming inwardly when she reached Marge's house, but within minutes the mundane problems of jobs and ex-husbands were largely banished. Cindy, who had begun to worry when Shelbie and Matt hadn't arrived quite when they had promised, had the door open for them before they were halfway up the walk from the cars. Even Huntzie, the cat with the eucalyptus-tree tail, came trotting out of another room to see what was going on, and then settled down on the back of a couch by the window to observe the proceedings.

Shelbie didn't explain why it had taken them so long to get there, only that they had been "held up." She knew that if she told Marge what she had discovered about C.G., the next regular issue of the *Bugle* would have a front-page editorial—probably libelous—concerning the town's foremost male chauvinist, although such mild terms would probably never be used. And Shelbie didn't want to get into that sort of battle—not right now, at least. Not until she had consulted with a lawyer or two, just to see what legal recourse, if any, she might have.

Marge was still at the dining room table, banging out the last of the filler items she needed to round out the "Suicide Special" issue of the *Bugle*. The rest of the copy was already pasted up, complete with clangorous headlines, ready for the printer. Marge's sixteen-year-old, Tim, seemed to be alternating between kibitzing over his mother's shoulder as she typed and doing his best to make sure Cindy was too frightened to even stick her head out the door after dark. She had already been apprehensive when she had talked to Shelbie and Matt earlier, but now she was beginning to wish she had not dug the stories out of the old *Sentinel*s in the first place.

"Obviously the epidemics are connected," Tim was saying over the clatter of the typewriter as Shelbie and the rest came within range. He was holding one of the paste-ups in his hand. "You're being much too cautious, Mother, saying there's only an 'apparent' connection."

"Obvious to you, maybe," his mother tossed back at him without breaking her stride on the typewriter, "but not so obvious to ordinary people. And if it's so obvious, then what *is* the connection? I've still got two or three column-inches I can spare if you would care to put in a theory."

Tim looked around and saw Cindy and the others then. He grinned. "Like I've been telling Cindy, there's *something* lurking around Elwood that's causing all these suicides. Something that—that surfaces every twenty years or so."

"All right, if you've got it all figured out," Marge began, but then she saw Shelbie herself, and she stopped typing and snatched the pages of paste-up from Tim. "Shel! You made it! Great! Here, take a look at these; see if you have any ideas." She grabbed the other pages from the littered tabletop and shoved them toward Shelbie. "After all, you're the one who started all this, so to speak. You don't mind getting credit for it, do you?" Marge pointed at one of the front-page columns.

"As long as you explain to the sheriff that I wasn't the one who let you in on everything. He's not going to be at all happy with any of this."

Marge waved a hand as if to erase the words and the problem from the air. "Don't worry about Lou," she said. "His bark is worse— But you know that saying as well as I do. Besides, I already told him that I had to sneak around behind your back to pry the information out of your assistant. Not that it took much prying."

Shelbie skimmed through the articles, passing the sheets to Matt as she finished. Despite the well-lighted room, the people around her, and the clattering of the typewriter, much of the mood she had felt earlier had returned. Typing and joking past the graveyard, she told herself, but she still found herself glancing uneasily toward the windows every few seconds. Finally, irritated with herself and envious of Marge's ability to ignore the problem altogether, Shelbie deliberately turned her back on the windows while she read the last pages of the articles.

All in all, the articles were factual enough, listing the sixteen suicides in the three epidemics, although Shelbie wasn't sure how much of the background on each of the victims was accurate. Most of it looked as if it had been taken from the original *Sentinel* articles, then slanted and expanded drastically, apparently with the major purpose of showing how unlikely, if not impossible, it was for any of these people to have killed themselves under "normal" circumstances. The only outright speculation, labeled as such, was the one that had been jokingly suggested when the second epidemic had first been discovered: a long-lived Jack the Ripper who caused "suicides." Assuming he had started young back at the time of the first epidemic, he —or she—could conceivably be as young as seventy now. The articles also mentioned the possibility of a family's being responsible, pointing out that to some severely warped minds, multiple murders might be looked on as some sort of rite marking the coming of adulthood. The periods between epidemics, approximately twenty-five years in both cases, certainly fit. Other "long-term mass murderers" were also invoked, such as Belle Gunness, who had done in at least ten suitors and hired hands over a period of several years, burying them all quietly in her barnyard outside LaPorte, Indiana, back in the early nineteen-hundreds.

"You don't mention the pewter monstrosity," Matt said as he scanned the last page that Shelbie had just handed him.

Marge looked toward him quickly. "You mean that thing you were asking me about yesterday? Don't tell me that's mixed up in this, too!"

Tim looked around interestedly as Matt shrugged. "Who knows? My uncle had one. Willy Brockman had one. Carla Schaeffer had one."

Marge frowned as she glanced at the others. "Nobody told

me about that. A cult of some sort, you mean? They leave these things behind to show they're responsible?"

Matt shook his head. "Not likely, certainly not in my uncle's case. He had his for at least twenty-odd years."

"Aha!" Tim broke in. "A witches' coven, or *some* kind of black magic practitioners!"

"Tim!" Cindy protested with a shudder, which was undoubtedly just the reaction he had been looking for.

"Sure," Tim went on, watching Cindy out of the corner of his eye, "those little figures must be like those dolls they use in voodoo."

Marge shook her head. "Come on, Tim, you're reaching. Pewter's soft, but not that soft. You'd never get a pin stuck in one of those."

"Who said you had to stick pins in them?" Tim asked. "That's only one kind of voodoo. Besides, I didn't say this *was* voodoo, just that those figures must have some magical significance. Anyway, Mom, you never do mention them in any of the articles, not even once. Don't you think you should?"

Marge frowned thoughtfully for a moment, then said, "Just a mention, maybe, but none of this supernatural nonsense. That would be overdoing it—for now, at least. Next thing you know, you'll be blaming it on UFOs. People would think I was putting out a comic book, not a newspaper. Not that some of them don't already think that." She looked at Shelbie. "But a picture, maybe. It was an ugly-looking little monster, from what I remember. We could mention in the caption that a figure like this one was in the possession of at least three of the victims. That might go over all right. Just another little hint of mystery, without trying to explain it to death. You wouldn't happen to have a picture of that thing, would you, Shel?"

Shelbie shook her head. "No, but you have a Polaroid, don't you?"

"Sure. With a half-tone screening doojigger, so I can use the pictures directly. But the little monster . . . You don't have that with you?"

"No, but it's easy enough to get from the museum. Or you could go down there and take a shot of it, if you want."

Marge hesitated, but only for an instant. "Sure, why not? Hang on a minute while I dig the camera out."

Tim was beaming happily as Marge disappeared into another room to look for the camera. "Now, when we print this picture," he said, "we'll probably hear from the relatives of all these other people. You want to bet that every one of them had one of those things? If it wasn't witches, it maybe was one of those secret societies."

"Doesn't sound like much of a society," Cindy said, still nervously, "if its members all kill themselves in their twenties. Besides, I don't know about the rest of them, but Carla would never join anything like that."

"You never know," Tim said, apparently trying to sound profound. "You'd never think she would kill herself, either."

Before anyone could respond, Marge was back, an old Polaroid dangling from one hand.

"Ready, Shelbie? Want to go in my car?"

"We can take mine," Shelbie said. "It's on the street already."

"Fine. Now, Tim, while we're gone, you do some rearranging of the copy. Shift things around so there'll be room for the picture on the front page—say, the lower-right corner, approximately. And leave room for five or six lines of caption."

"Sure, Mom." Tim was already sitting down at the typewriter. "I'll write up a caption, too. You can—"

Marge turned back to Tim. "Okay. But just remember—be subtle. Don't beat them over the head with it. And don't mess around with the stuff you're moving to make room. Just move it, don't change it. Understood?"

"Sure, Mom, but—"

"No buts. Cindy, you keep an eye on him. And Matt—are you staying here or coming with us?"

Once they got outside, they decided to take Matt's Checker instead of Shelbie's Toyota, and Marge insisted on getting into

the mammoth back seat by herself, leaning back and stretching
her legs out full-length in front of her.

"Should've had one of these the time I was driving the gover-
nor and his buddies around," she mused. "How old *is* this
thing? It looks like a fifty-five Chevy."

"It's only three or four years old," Matt said, "but you're
right. Back in the fifties was the last time they changed the
style."

Marge laughed. "Beautiful. Never goes out of style, but on
the other hand, it's never in style in the first place." She looked
around the back seat again, speculatively. "Wonder if I could
get one of these things secondhand for a few bucks. I could just
about get the entire press run of the *Bugle* in the back seat
here."

Then they were at the museum. Matt ignored the lot and
parked in the alley a few feet from the door. Shelbie dug out
her key and went to the door, flanked by Matt and Marge.

"Haven't been in here since I quit the society," Marge said as
Shelbie inserted the key in the lock. "Got everything out on display yet?"

Shelbie shook her head. "Hardly. We've still got two or three
basements and a couple of attics full of things. And we still
haven't gotten that old box wagon restored."

Shelbie frowned as she pushed at the door and it didn't
move.

"Something wrong?" Matt asked.

"Trouble with the key, that's all." She tried the door again,
then put the key back in and twisted it once more. There was a
click, and when she tried the knob again, the door opened normally.

"Wrong key the first time?" Marge asked.

Shelbie stood silently for a moment, not entering the darkened interior. The only light, aside from the faint rectangle cast
through the door by the distant street lamp, was the dull
reddish glow from the exit sign. A feeling of uneasiness was
gradually taking hold of her again.

"I don't think so," Shelbie said. "It just didn't open the first time. It was as if—"

She stopped, blinking, and looked down at the key, trying to remember which way she had turned it the first time, but she couldn't. She never could. When she unlocked a door, she simply put the key in and tried turning it one way or the other. If it didn't turn on the first try, she simply twisted it the other way. And this time, all she could remember was that the key *had* turned the first time. And yet the door hadn't opened. It had still been locked.

Or, in turning the key, she could have locked it herself—if it had been unlocked to begin with. If Cindy, in her rush to get away to join Marge and Tim after their discovery of the third epidemic . . .

"Well, are you just going to stand there all night?" Marge asked. "Or do we go inside one of these days?"

Shelbie glanced around, pushing her speculations away but unable to rid herself of the uneasiness.

"Sorry," she said, pushing the door open the rest of the way. "I was just wondering about that lock. I'd better have someone look at it one of these days. It doesn't seem to be working right."

She flipped on the switch next to the door, and the fluorescents flickered into life overhead.

Marge looked around appreciatively as Shelbie led the way through the first room, past the farm implements and display cases and eighteen-nineties kitchen. "Hey, Shel, this is really something!" Marge said. "You really *do* have a lot of room. I never thought we'd have enough space to set up all that barnyard junk."

"It's mostly your doing, don't forget," Shelbie said. "You're the one who talked the council into renting this place."

Marge brushed the compliment aside the same way she erased problems out of the air with her hand. "Got anything I can use for a backdrop? Some black cloth? A dark pillow? Anything like that?"

"I think so," Shelbie said. "Would some black artboard work? I think there's a sheet in one of the cabinets."

"Sure, that would be fine." Marge looked around the inner room as the fluorescents came on. "Now, I also need a light, something besides those things up there in the ceiling. Something—something like your desk light. That should work okay, if we can move it around a little."

"Help yourself to anything you need," Shelbie told her. "The artboard is in that cabinet back in the corner, I think. It's not locked, so you take a look while I—"

Shelbie stopped abruptly as she turned toward the display case and glanced down. For an instant she thought she might be looking at the wrong case, but that possibility was pushed out of her mind almost immediately as her eyes darted across the other displays—the meerschaum carving, the photo album, the cameo, and all the other case's residents. No, it was the right display case, she realized, and with that realization, the uneasiness that had lain coiled within her since she had approached the museum door suddenly blossomed into fear.

"It's gone," she said, her voice, though little more than a whisper, seeming to echo back from the bare walls. "The figure is gone."

CHAPTER 13

Matt, who had been standing in the archway to the outer room, hurried across the floor toward Shelbie. Marge turned sharply from the cabinet she had just opened.

"What's gone?" Marge asked loudly from across the room. "Not the little monster, I hope."

Shelbie nodded, her eyes still fastened on the vacant spot in the display case. The door *had* been unlocked when she had first put the key in it, she thought. Someone *had* been in here.

But to break in and steal only a pewter figure, something that was worthless to anyone but the historical society . . . It just didn't make sense. But then, nothing that had happened in the last two days had really made sense, she told herself.

Then Matt was standing beside her, his hands on her arms. He looked down at the vacant spot in the case, and Shelbie could feel his fingers tighten on her arms.

"What happened to it?" he asked. "Are you sure you put it back in there this afternoon? We were doing a lot of rushing around there for a while."

Shelbie shook her head. "I put it back. And I *think* the door was unlocked when we arrived just now."

"Somebody stole it?" Marge had moved across the room and was standing next to Matt. "Who on earth would want something like that?"

"I don't know," Matt said, releasing Shelbie's arms after a final, reassuring squeeze, "but we'd better call the sheriff. And Shelbie, you'd better check and make sure nothing else is missing."

Marge muttered a couple of curses about the burglar's rotten timing, then looked at Shelbie. "I'd better call Tim and tell him to forget about shifting things around to make room for a picture. Unless you happen to have another of them around. Didn't you say there were three of the monsters?"

Shelbie shook her head as Matt picked up the telephone to call the sheriff's office. "Just two that I've seen," she said. "The one that Matt's uncle had may be the same one that Carla had."

"But there is at least one more?" Marge persisted. "Who's got it now?"

"The sheriff. At least, he had it when we left him this afternoon."

"Well, maybe I'm still in business." Marge turned and hurried over to Matt, who was still talking into the phone. "Tell him to bring the little monster with him when he comes over," she said, tapping him heavily on the shoulder.

Matt nodded and, after a minute, relayed the message. As he hung up, he looked at Marge. "You're lucky," he said. "That was Dick Reynolds, not Lou. Anyway, he said he'd bring the thing over."

Marge grinned. "Well, things may work out after all. Now, Shel, can I use your desk to take the pictures? I think if I cover up all the papers with the backdrop, I can swivel your desk light around enough to get the right lighting . . ."

By the time Dick arrived, neither Matt nor Shelbie had thought of any reason for the figure to have been stolen, and Shelbie had not been able to find anything else missing or even disturbed. If was as if the intruder had unlocked the door, gone straight to the display case, taken the figure out, and left, neglecting only to lock the door behind him.

Marge, on the other hand, used the time to get set up to take her pictures. The backdrop was in place, and she had been using another figure—a miniature bust of one of Elwood's founding fathers—to get the light the way she wanted it. When Dick arrived, she took the figure from him and started to work, ignoring everything else.

After a few questions which netted him no worthwhile information, Dick opened the fingerprint kit he had brought with him and dusted the entire back of the display case.

There was nothing—not a single print—not even Shelbie's or Cindy's. Nor was there anything to be found on the door to the outside, except for a couple of smudges that looked like Shelbie's, although Dick couldn't tell for sure.

"Looks like whoever it was wiped everything he touched." Dick looked down at the fingerprint kit and sighed. "You still can't think of anything else that's missing?" he asked.

"Nothing."

"What about the other break-in, the one a couple of weeks ago? There was nothing at all missing or disturbed that time, was there?"

"Not a thing." Shelbie glanced toward the desk where Marge was snapping another picture of the pewter figure. The fear Shelbie had felt when she had first seen the figure was missing had diminished, but it had never gone fully away, and ever since Dick had brought in the near-duplicate figure, all the other feelings of the evening had been milling around inside her like a hundred lead-footed butterflies. And every so often, whenever one of the periodic silences would fall over everyone, or whenever she would glance at the darkened windows, a shiver would float along her spine for a moment, and she would think once again, involuntarily: All these things can't be coincidence. *Something* out there is making them happen!

And every so often her eyes would be drawn to the figure itself, and the shiver would be renewed. Tim's wild theories about witches and voodoo were nonsense, of course. Tim himself knew that; he was only trying to scare Cindy—and probably anyone else that he could, or maybe even himself. But still, there must be *some* connection. No matter what her rational mind said, that figure—or another one very much like it—had been in the possession of at least three unexplained suicides. That much was fact, and it took a great deal of coincidence to explain it away.

And now someone had broken into the museum and stolen one of the figures.

No sense. It made no sense at all. No more sense than Ben Cunningham's disposing of nearly half a million dollars in a matter of weeks, and then killing himself. No more sense than Willy Brockman's doing the same thing a quarter of a century earlier.

Suddenly a thought struck Shelbie. Tim had talked about a secret society, something mystical and mysterious. What if it *were* true? She couldn't imagine what the nature of such a society might be, but with that much money disappearing, not once but twice—

She shook her head sharply, tearing her eyes away from the pewter figure, still lying on the black backdrop on her desk. The odd way Marge had the thing lighted, it seemed to be looking at her, as if, hidden in the shadowed hollows beneath the inhumanly prominent brows, there really was a pair of eyes.

Dick looked up from closing his fingerprint kit. "Not much else I can do here, I'm afraid. You want to come down in the morning and fill out an official report on what's missing?"

Shelbie looked toward him. Matt was standing not far from the desk, watching Marge finish the pictures. "All right," she said.

"And I would suggest you get the lock changed on that door. From the looks of it, it was simply opened with a key," Dick said. "At least I couldn't find anything to indicate it had been forced."

"I will," Shelbie said, then added, "although I'm not completely sure the door wasn't left unlocked this time."

"And that other time? A couple of weeks ago?"

"It's possible it was left unlocked then, too. But you're right. I'll get the lock changed."

Dick nodded and walked over to Marge. "Mrs. Remington? Are you about finished? I really should take that back with me."

Marge looked around, the last of the Polaroid shots in her hand. In the wastebasket next to the desk were the discarded negative-halves of a dozen others.

"Just about done," she said after a quick look at the camera.

"I've only got a couple of pictures left in the camera, so I've got to be through. I still don't have the right lighting, though. Hey, Shel, you want to give me a hand? Or an eye, rather? Didn't you used to fool around with a camera now and then?"

"Fool around is about right," Shelbie said, shrugging off the shivery feeling that still played around her spine. "What's the trouble?"

"How should I know?" Marge shrugged broadly. "If I knew what the trouble was, I'd fix it myself. Here, take a look at what I've got so far."

Marge handed her a half dozen shots, and Matt passed over another batch that he had been looking at. Shelbie glanced through them quickly, nervously. Most were full-face shots, though a few were three-quarter, one even a profile. None were really bad, although in a couple of the full-face shots, you couldn't tell what the thing looked like, not unless you already knew.

"How about this one?" Shelbie asked, holding out one of the clearer full-face shots.

"If I can't get anything better, that's the one I'll go with. But it just isn't what I'm after. Wrong shadows or something."

"I really should be getting back to the office," Dick said. He was standing by patiently but was beginning to look nervous about the delay. "Sam's sick tonight, so there's no one there to even answer the phone."

For a moment, as Shelbie's eyes went from the photo to Dick's face, the coldness seemed to launch a new attack, flowing over her back like a wave of chilled, basement-damp air. And out of the corner of her eye, she saw Matt wince slightly—as if he, too, were being affected. Impossible, of course, but . . .

Then, without being fully aware of what words were going to come out, she said, "Look, Dick, why don't you go on back. I'll look after the—the figure. I'll drop it off whenever we get finished here. All right?"

"I really shouldn't, Shelbie." He looked at her uncertainly, then at the figure, and she wondered if it could possibly be making him nervous, too. "All right, Shelbie," he said quickly. "You can keep it for a while. But don't forget—you're bringing it back to the office as soon as you're finished."

"I won't forget; don't worry."

"Thanks, Shel," Marge said when Dick had left. "But I've still got only two pictures left, no matter how long we keep the thing. And there's no place at this time of night to buy film that I know of."

Without answering, Shelbie reached out and picked the figure up. The chill along her spine, now probing forward into her stomach, remained unabated, and it was all she could do to keep from spinning around to look behind her.

The feeling, the sense of another presence hovering in the room with them, watching silently, invisibly, was stronger than ever.

But there *was* no one! There was herself. There was Marge. And there was Matt.

And there was the pewter figure . . .

Sharply, she shook her head, pressed her eyes tightly shut for a second.

"Here," she said, laying the figure back on the backdrop. She was sure that, no matter how hard she tried, her voice must be reflecting her nervousness. "Marge, you keep an eye on it through the viewfinder, and I'll move the desk lamp around, okay? You tell me when I have it in the right place, when you're getting the kind of shadows you want."

Despite Shelbie's help, the last two pictures came out no closer to what Marge thought she was after than the first dozen had. Marge shrugged as she looked at the last one and tossed the sticky brown negative into the wastebasket.

"Might as well put away my junk and get back to the house," she said. "They're probably wondering what happened to us."

As it turned out, Cindy had been wondering, but Tim had barely realized they were gone. He had moved the pasted-up copy around quickly enough, leaving space for the photo, and now he had over half a dozen different captions written for it, all of which Marge quickly and decisively vetoed. She sat down then and, after a few seconds of thoughtful silence, batted out a caption of her own.

It was almost two o'clock when everyone was finally satisfied with the final product, although Tim was still complaining about not being allowed to include a paragraph or two about the theft of the figure from the museum and some of his pet theories. Finally, though, the least objectionable of the Polaroids was pasted in place, and everything broke up for the night. As Cindy drove away, glad for once that her mother always left two or three lights burning until she got home, Shelbie and Matt stood by their cars silently, neither making a move to get in.

Finally Matt said, "You never did find those manuscripts you wanted me to take a look at."

Shelbie glanced at her wristwatch in the dim light from the street lamp fifty feet away. "You wouldn't get anything done on them tonight anyway, unless you've got insomnia."

"Which I may have, after everything that's been going on tonight." He shook his head, ran his fingers through his uncombed hair. "But I can stop and pick them up in the morning, if you like."

"Yes, that might be better."

They stood silently again, their eyes not quite meeting. The uneasiness, the sense of another presence, still hovered over Shelbie, and it was still all she could do to keep from darting a look behind her. Most of the houses in the neighborhood were dark, and the only sound, other than a faint wind through the trees that lined the street, was that of Cindy's car, distant and fading. The clouds that had moved in late in the afternoon still filled the sky, blocking out the moon and stars alike.

Shelbie looked up, her eyes meeting Matt's, and she wondered where the feeling between them—the feeling of "comfort"—had gone. But then, as she thought of it consciously for the first time in hours, she realized that it was still there, buried somewhere within her. It had been swamped by the other feelings, by the persistent, chilling "presence" that continued to bring a tingle to her spine even now.

Abruptly, she wondered: Does he feel it, too?

And just as abruptly, she saw the answer, as clearly as if he had spoken the words: He does.

"How long?" she asked, as much with her eyes and face as with the words.

For just a moment, his eyes widened, but then his features relaxed, his shoulders slumped a fraction, and he let his breath out in a faint sigh.

"I first noticed it yesterday morning, when I came into the museum and saw the—the figure. I thought at first it was simply because I recognized it from when I was a kid. I thought it was just curiosity, and maybe a 'hunch' about what happened to my uncle and his money."

"But now?" Shelbie prompted when he fell silent, his eyes wandering over the darkness around them, searching.

He shook his head as his eyes came back to her face. "Now? Now I don't know, any more than you do."

Again his eyes moved restlessly over the darkness, and he hunched his shoulders as if against a nonexistent coldness in the air. "All I know is, I want to look over my shoulder every five seconds. I know there's nothing there, but— Is that how it is with you?"

She nodded, and again there was silence between them. They both knew that there was no explanation either of them could make that would help, no guesses that would comfort them. There was nothing rational that could account for what had been happening in Elwood for the last fifty years, perhaps longer. And there was nothing rational that could account for the way they both felt now, for the way they seemed to almost read each other's thoughts and emotions. Nothing rational . . .

And yet, there had to be *something* to account for it all.

Something that would account for more than a dozen suicides by people who had no reasons for killing themselves.

Something that would account for the disappearance of at least two fortunes under conditions that were unlikely, to say the least.

Something that would account for an aging pewter figure

being owned—or at least possessed—by three or more of the
suicides at the time of death.

And something that would account for the impossible, shared
feeling that someone or something was nearby . . .

Suddenly, Shelbie reached out, and just as suddenly, she felt
the warmth and comfort of Matt's arms around her and the
solidness of his body within her own arms. No words were
spoken, but no words were needed. Each knew what the other
felt, and each knew that, except in the most superficial way,
words could not express it. And each knew that, for this moment, they drew strength and comfort from each other, that
each contributed and profited equally, that together they had a
chance against whatever madness hovered over them. The feeling, the chill of knowing that, somewhere in the darkness, invisible eyes watched their every move and thought, was not
banished; but its power over them was broken, just as the
power of a darkened bedroom is broken when a child wraps
the covers tightly about himself and wriggles his back into the
mattress beneath him. For the moment, there is safety.

Then, still wordlessly, it was over. Slowly, they released each
other and stepped back. Some small part of the warmth and
comfort remained, as if, by the simple expedient of touching, a
permanent link had been formed.

For several seconds, they stood silently facing each other.
Then Matt held out his hand, and Shelbie knew, without his
having to speak, what he wanted.

Slowly, she reached into her purse and brought out the pewter figure, the nightmare features barely registering in her mind.
She laid it in Matt's outstretched hand.

Shelbie knew the figure would not be returned to the sheriff's
office tonight. . . .

It was a voice, and yet not a voice.

It told him to awaken, and yet it held his mind in an unbreakable grip.

It spoke as if from a great distance, and yet it seemed to come from within himself, the thoughts to form of their own accord in his mind.

It spoke of endless life, and yet a taint of death hovered over its words.

It spoke of fulfillment of all desires, and yet there was a tinge of emptiness and eternal loneliness to the thoughts.

It was touched by an aura of alienness that, when his thoughts were his own, hinted at unknown forms and terrors, and yet, almost from the start, he accepted what it seemed to be offering.

Gradually, as the night wore on, he changed. . . .

CHAPTER 14

In the morning, the sun was again shining, and Shelbie was rationalizing her actions of the night before, both her seemingly easy acceptance of the impossible and her sudden leap into Matt's arms.

Everything, it seemed, had conspired against her in both areas. The minor trauma of losing the job and the major trauma of finding out why she had lost it. The year and a half she had spent being cautious—even wary—about any serious involvement with a man for fear that, under the surface, he would turn out to be another C.G. Marge's special "suicide edition," not to mention Tim's wild theories, even the atmosphere of the museum itself late at night. And, of course, the theft of the figure.

But now, in the sunlight of the morning after, it was all obviously impossible. Believing in strange, insubstantial "feelings" and in "epidemics" of suicides was little better than the insanity she had already had occasional qualms about. And to believe that there was any "mystical bond" between herself and Matt Decker, even temporarily . . .

To complete her conversion from the unrealities of the night to the realities of the day, she even went so far as turn on "Today" on her miniature kitchen-table TV set while she fixed herself a couple of slices of raisin-bread toast and nibbled at a wedge of farmer's cheese. The news, however, turned out to be simply a different kind of insanity, a public, worldwide brand which would, she realized, be just as hard to accept as her own private brand if she had not had a lifetime to become accustomed to the public variety. And to make things completely perfect, the weather forecast predicted that rain would replace the clear, warm skies by late evening.

She was about to close the door and start down the steps when the phone rang. It had rung once last night after she had gotten back, but knowing that it would probably be Dick Reynolds wondering politely what had happened to the pewter figure he had lent her, she hadn't answered. Wondering how she would be able to explain it now, even to herself, she crossed the room and picked up the receiver.

But it was Matt, not Dick, and after only the briefest of greetings, he said: "Shelbie, we have to find them all—every single one."

For a moment, her mind was blank, and she wanted to ask what he was talking about, but before she could form the words, she knew. In an instant, the last six hours, the rationalizations, the logic, were all gone. All she could see in her mind's eyes was the face—the demonic face of the pewter figure as Matt's hand had closed over it the night before.

"Why?" she asked.

There was a pause, and she could imagine him running his fingers nervously through his hair as he drew in his breath to speak. "I don't know," he said, "not for sure. Not logically, anyway. It's like that hunch or whatever when I saw the first one in the museum. If I find the figures, I'll find the money—or at least I'll find out what happened to it. And don't ask me why I think so. Or how I expect to find them, or how many there are. I don't know. I just don't know!"

"You still have the figure? You didn't return it to Dick last night?"

"I still have it. Are you in trouble because of it?"

"I don't think so. I haven't heard from Dick yet this morning, so . . ." Her voice trailed away, and her mind moved inexorably back to the pewter figure. "What do we do first?" she asked.

Another pause. "I'll meet you at Marge Remington's," he said finally. "She and her son seemed just as interested in—in

finding out what was going on as we were. And that article of
hers had a list of several of the relatives of the suicide victims."

Hold on a second, a rational corner of her mind interrupted.
One of these days, you've got to get back to the everyday business of the historical society, especially now that you've lost out
in Argos. Business like the unedited articles and autobi-
ographies for volume two of *Farrell County Folks,* which—

"What about your volunteer editing work?" Shelbie asked
abruptly. "Still interested?"

"Editing? Oh, you mean those—" He paused, apparently uneasy at the sudden switch in topics. "Yes, I guess I still am. But
this other . . . Look, why don't you bring them with you? I'll
take them along, and whenever I get a chance—whenever this
other thing is over . . ."

Marge Remington was just returning from the printer when
Shelbie arrived at her house.

"Five thousand copies by this evening, at the latest," Marge
said, grinning. "Orin promised. And then comes the hard part
—selling them. Do you still have any pull at the *Sentinel,* Shel?
Enough to get me a cut-rate ad for my special edition?"

Shelbie smiled, but a twinge of bitterness jabbed at her stomach. "Hardly," she said. "The way things are going, C.G. would
probably charge you double if I tried to put in a good word for
you. But what I want to talk to you about is Matt, not C.G.
Matt and our pewter monsters."

"Oh?" Marge cocked her head sideways quizzically. "Something new?"

"Maybe. The thing is, Matt thinks those pewter figures are
the key to—well, to lots of things. At least the key to what happened to Ben Cunningham's money."

Marge's eyes widened. "You're starting to sound like Tim.
But I suppose now that someone's gone to the trouble of breaking into the museum and stealing one of them, his wild ideas
may not be so wild after all. But does Matt have *any* idea
what's *really* going on?"

Shelbie shook her head. "He didn't say, and I know that *I*

certainly don't. It's probably just a—" She stopped, not wanting to say the word but unable to think of any other.

"A hunch?" Marge supplied for her. "Yeah, I know what you mean. But how can I help you?"

"Your special issue. You have the names of all the victims, plus capsule biographies and lists of survivors."

Marge nodded. "I don't vouch for accuracy, though. I picked up all that stuff out of the original obituaries in the *Sentinel*. All I did was embellish a bit."

Shelbie grinned. "I thought so. But the point is, you have all the names in one place, including surviving members of the families. We'd like to get a copy so Matt and I can talk to a few of them today."

"Sure. All I have is the manuscript, though, and I don't dare let that out of my hands until I get the printed copies back this evening. You know how a print shop can chew things up if you give them half a chance and forget to keep the manuscript. But if you'd like to copy the names down, I'll give you a hand." Marge paused, looked thoughtful for a moment. "In fact," she went on, "I'll even help you talk to some people. Maybe we'll come up with enough for another special *Bugle*."

They were almost finished with their copying when Matt arrived a few minutes later.

"If anyone asks," he said to Shelbie, "the sheriff's office has loaned you the pewter figure as a temporary replacement for the one that was stolen last night. At least that's the best story I could get Dick to agree to when he called me last night."

Shelbie looked up from her copying. "So that's why he didn't call me again."

Matt nodded. "He said he tried to reach you, but you must not have gotten home yet."

"I was home, I just didn't answer the phone. I was sure it was him, and I knew what he wanted. The only thing I didn't know was what I would tell him about the way you wandered off with that thing last night." She frowned briefly. "Why *did* you take it with you? Why didn't you give it back to Dick?"

A faint smile touched his broad features for a moment.

"Why didn't *you* give it back to him? After all, you're the one who borrowed it in the first place."

"Because you took it with you," she said lamely.

"And you knew I wasn't planning to return it, didn't you?"

Reluctantly, she nodded. So much for rationality in the sunlit morning.

Marge stood up then, shoving her completed list across the kitchen table to Shelbie. "Maybe Tim was right," she said. "Maybe it *is* a voodoo idol of some sort. It sure has got the two of you hexed. Now that you've got it, what are you planning to do with it?"

Shelbie picked up the lists she and Marge had made out. "Show it to all the people we talk to, I assume. Right, Matt? See if they remember ever seeing anything like it before?"

Matt nodded. "It's the only way I can think of to find the—the rest of them."

Marge looked at him curiously. "The rest of what? The monsters? How many are there supposed to be?"

Matt only shook his head. "Maybe we'll have a better idea after we've talked to some of these people."

"If you say so. But what I still don't get is why you're looking for them at all. Shel said something about them having something to do with your uncle's missing money—maybe. What *is* the connection?"

"I haven't the faintest idea," Matt admitted. He shook his head irritably. "All I know is, looking for them seemed like a good idea when it first occurred to me last night. And it still does!" he finished defiantly.

"Another hunch?" Marge asked.

"I suppose. I know it doesn't make any sense, but I've already taken all the logical steps I can think of, and they've gotten me absolutely nowhere. Except in debt to a private detective agency and a lawyer. There's nothing left for me now *but* hunches. Or delusions."

Shelbie started to deny that they were delusions, but she couldn't—not with any conviction. The fact that, to a point, she shared the hunches—or delusions—didn't help.

"Anyway," Marge was saying, "you really do think that if you find out more about these—these pewter monsters, you'll find out what happened to your uncle's missing money?"

Matt laughed, a trifle harshly. "Who knows? Certainly not me. I *feel* it, but—"

Once again he shook his head, as if trying to clear it. "It's—it's like a contest, a lottery. You *know* the odds are a thousand or a million to one against you, but when you watch the guy pull the winning number out of the drum, there's always a second, just before he reads it, that you *know* he's going to read off your number. But he never does, and you know he isn't going to this time either. . . . It's the same thing here, probably. I *want* to believe my number is coming up, so some perverse corner of my mind keeps telling me it *is* coming up, whether there's a chance that it really is or not. And that stupid statue or whatever it is is something I associate with my uncle, and therefore with the money. . . ." He shrugged. "How's that for instant and ridiculous self-analysis?"

"Not bad," Marge said. "But aren't hunches sometimes based on something your subconscious mind knows but your conscious mind doesn't?"

Matt shrugged. "It would be nice to think so, at least this time around. Preferable to thinking I'm going bananas, at any rate. But even if it's true, the problem is to drag that hypothetical knowledge out of my subconscious and into the light where I can see it. Right? Any suggestions? Or do we just keep on thrashing around the way we have been?"

"Hypnosis?" Marge asked. "That's supposed to let you unearth all sorts of buried memories, isn't it?"

Matt hesitated, then shook his head. "Can't say I care for the idea. Maybe someday, after everything else has failed . . ." Again he hesitated, grinned faintly. "Besides, I've got a hunch it wouldn't work."

By the end of the day, they had found out several things, all disturbing but none really surprising. And nothing they discovered seemed to bring them any closer to finding the other pewter figures—assuming there really were others—or to discovering what had happened to Ben Cunningham's money or why he—or any of the others—had committed suicide.

They talked to a half dozen people who knew or had been related to the current crop of suicides. One of them—Elvon Baker's sister, Betty Van Duyne—did remember seeing a "little statue" that she thought looked quite a lot like the pewter figure. She couldn't be sure, of course, but whatever it was she had seen had been lying, of all places, on the bureau in Elvon's bedroom. The only reason she remembered it at all was that Elvon "never went in for knickknacks or anything like that." She hadn't seen it since then and had no idea what had happened to it.

They talked to three relatives of the previous group, the ones who had killed themselves in 1951. One of them, too, remembered seeing something similar to the pewter figure. Harry Radtke, Arthur Radtke's father, now well into his seventies, remembered it because he had found it on the porch of his son's house just before he found his son's body. The figure had apparently been thrown through the closed window and had struck the porch railing. He had carried it inside, he remembered, but had dropped it when he saw his son's body. He never saw the figure again, and his only theory about it was that his son had changed his mind about killing himself after he had taken the pills but had been unable to get off the bed and had thrown the figure through the window in an effort to draw attention. He had no idea what had happened to the figure after he dropped it when he saw the body of his son.

By sheer luck, they found a relative of Rebecca Emrick, the woman who had led off the 1926 epidemic. It was her sister's granddaughter, but they found out very little from her. All Jessica Cross remembered about her great-aunt was that "the old gal didn't have as much money as everybody thought." Or so Jessica's grandmother, Rebecca's sister, had said, often and bitterly over the years.

"It *could* mean that Rebecca did the same thing that Brockman and my uncle did," Matt said when they left the Cross apartment, and Shelbie couldn't bring herself to argue against the idea.

The most disturbing news, however, came not from talking to friends or relatives of the suicides but from Tim's further research in the library's files of the *Elwood Sentinel*.

He found two more suicide epidemics, one in 1905 and one in 1877.

CHAPTER 15

The pattern in the two newly discovered epidemics was the same as in the others: one middle-aged victim followed by several in their early or middle twenties—three in one case, seven in the other.

Shelbie could not keep from shivering as Tim outlined his discovery late that afternoon in the museum, particularly when he began to list the 1905 victims. The first was Josiah Wintergreen, who had built the Cunningham house in 1885. Cindy, though, was the most upset of anyone, and before Tim had a chance to do more than run through the list of names, she shuddered openly, gathered up her purse, and left.

"I'll be having enough nightmares as it is," she said as she virtually ran from the room.

Surprisingly, Tim did not give her a parting shot to even further increase her chances of nightmares, and Shelbie noticed that the boy's normally enthusiastic manner was relatively subdued. In telling them what he had found, he had not editorialized or speculated wildly. He had simply given them the names and dates.

And now, as the door in the outer room clanked shut behind Cindy, he made no joke, no comment, only glanced toward his mother. Finally, a nervous grin pulled at his lips.

"I'll be having nightmares myself if this keeps up much longer," he said. "What do we do now?"

Nobody had any constructive ideas. They would tell the sheriff, of course, but no one expected anything to result from that. The most that could happen would be that he might consent to having a picture of the pewter figure run in the *Sentinel*, along with an official request that anyone who found or saw anything resembling the figure report it to his office immediately. And he would make sure that his own daughter did not have one. But that would be all. And, they had to admit, it was all they could logically expect anyone to do. And it was all they could think of to do themselves. If the problem were something a bit less insane, like a local version of the Boston Strangler, something which people could see and believe in, perhaps something could be done. Doors could be locked. Lights could be left on. Strangers could be avoided. But this . . . Watch out for weird-looking little statues, and be careful that you don't commit suicide? A warning like that, even if it could be made, would provoke more laughs than caution.

Nor did they do much better in their speculations as to what might be behind it all. Tim, of course, had a number of ideas, mostly taken from the monster movies he was addicted to; but this time, unlike the night before, he seemed to be taking the speculations seriously, not scattergunning them in all directions.

"If they were out-and-out murders, it would be easy enough," he said at one point. "Easy to come up with fantasy solutions, anyway. There's always the old idea about Jack the Ripper or someone like that being an immortal who has to kill a batch of people every twenty years or so in order to retain his youth. But this . . ." He shrugged his bony shoulders, then brightened slightly as a new idea occurred to him. "Unless it's some kind of vampire—not the kind that sucks your blood but one that could siphon off your—your 'life force.'" He grinned sheepishly. "Whatever that might be."

"A lot of people believe in a soul," Matt said, "so why not a 'life force'? And when it's drained away, the person has no will to live, so he kills himself. And the vampire—or witch or whatever—goes on about his business."

Tim looked at Matt with a touch of surprise and admiration. "You're right—that *would* account for a lot. For all the young ones, at least. But what about the older ones? The first one to go in each epidemic has always been an older person."

Matt shook his head. "I was lucky to come up with even that much of an idea."

Tim frowned thoughtfully for a moment. "Maybe he has to work up to the younger ones?" he speculated. "Sort of an appetizer, so to speak. An older person wouldn't have as much life force left, so . . ."

"And the money?" Matt asked. "In the last three cases, the first and older suicide was fairly rich, and in two cases for sure —probably in all three—most of their money vanished when they died."

"So the vampire needs not only life force but money," Tim said, some of his earlier high spirits returning. "I always did wonder how Dracula and those other characters were able to keep up their castles the way they did, without any money ever coming in." He nodded. "Maybe that's why he takes an older, richer victim first each time. Of course that would mean he'd have to be doing more than simply draining out the victim's life force. He'd have to have some kind of control over him first, to make him convert his assets into cash and then give the cash to the vampire. . . ."

In the end, though, the speculation came to nothing, and they again decided the only practical thing they could do was to give Sheriff Rokane the facts the next morning and let it go at that. Even Matt seemed to have given up on trying to locate other pewter figures. And Tim, apparently deciding that life must go on, regardless of what hangs over one's head, borrowed his mother's car keys and departed for home to get cleaned up and ready for a date. Shelbie and Marge, at Matt's insistence, piled into his Checker, and he drove out to Cheyney's, a smorgasbord restaurant on the north shore of the lake. Buying them a meal was the least he could do, he explained, since most of the legwork they had been doing in the last two days had been because of his "hunch." Somehow, though, they avoided pewter figures and suicides as subjects of mealtime conversation. Most of the time, Marge told horror stories of a different kind, mostly about her two ex-husbands, both of whom were, to hear her tell it, at least as bad as C.G., with none of his redeeming features.

When they left the restaurant, the sun had just set into a bank of clouds, and it looked as if the morning's prediction of rain by late evening would prove true.

Marge glanced at her watch as they climbed into the Checker. "One more favor, Matt?" she asked.

"Sure, whatever you want." He backed the car out from between a pair of low-slung sports cars and maneuvered it toward the road.

"That special edition of the *Bugle* we put together last night is supposed to be ready by now," she said, "and Orin's print shop closes in a few minutes. Could we stop by and pick it up?"

"Just tell me where it is."

Marge gave directions, and in five minutes they were parked in the alley behind the print shop. Marge climbed out and hurried through the small back door into the concrete block building. She had been inside less than a minute when Shelbie heard Marge's voice. It was loud, angry, and unintelligible, muffled by the distance and the closed door to the building.

Then Marge reappeared, her stride long and firm, her lips clamped tightly together, her face a mask of fury. As she yanked open the back door of the Checker and threw herself inside, a man in an ink-stained apron appeared in the door, took a couple of steps toward the car, and halted.

"I'm sorry, Mrs. Remington," he said haltingly, "I'm truly sorry. But you've got to understand. I depend on—"

"I understand," Marge said tightly, not looking directly at the man. "I'm not blaming you, Orin."

The man in the ink-stained apron took another hesitant step toward the car and faltered to a stop again. His mouth opened, but no words came out.

"Let's go!" Marge snapped, and, puzzledly, Matt obeyed.

"What happened?" Shelbie asked, turning around in the front seat to look at Marge, who was pressing herself back into the corner of the huge back seat, her arms folded, her fingers drumming soundlessly.

Marge was silent except for her breath, which hissed in and out through still-clenched teeth. After several seconds, she looked at Shelbie.

"Your loving ex has just shafted *me,* too!" she said.

"C.G.? What's he got to do with Orin?"

"He gives him a fair amount of business, apparently, or at least steers a lot of business Orin's way," Marge said, biting off each word harshly. "And C.G. made it abundantly clear that if Orin printed any more *Bugle*s for me, that was the end of the steering!"

"What?" It was a shocked chorus from both Shelbie and Matt, and Shelbie went on. "Orin's been printing the *Bugle* ever since you started it."

"But not any more! Not if he wants to stay in your ex's good graces!"

"Why? What possible reason— Don't tell me he's suddenly afraid of the competition?"

"How should I know?" Marge shook her head, her dull orange-red hair flying. "But I *am* going to find out, right now!"

Matt had pulled the Checker over to the curb a block from the print shop, uncertain of their destination, and now he swiveled around to look at Marge. "Orin *told* you this? That Griggs ordered him not to print your paper?"

"Not only that, he left a message for me to 'come and see him' to talk about it when I had the chance! Can you believe the nerve of that—" She broke off, shaking her head.

Shelbie snorted loudly. "*I* can believe it. After what he did to me last night, I can believe anything. Anyone who would pull a stunt like that with the school board—" She broke off, purposely cutting short what could easily have become a tirade.

"But why?" Matt was shaking his head. "It doesn't make sense, not this. Your job, Shelbie—well, I can see some kind of warped, macho logic behind that, but this—"

"Let's find out," Marge said abruptly. "He said I should come and see him, so let's do just that!"

Shelbie's first thought was that it would be pointless. When C.G. thought he was right—*knew* he was right, rather—nothing would change his mind. Not logic, not persuasion, not anything. And to see him now, feeling the way she did, to have to listen to his condescending, chauvinistic "reasoning"— The best they could hope for would be a shouting match, with tempers cranked up even further.

But before Shelbie could formulate the words to go with her thoughts, a second thought came: Why not? it asked. Let's get it out in the open once and for all, with witnesses. One final confrontation, so we all know just exactly where we stand, so we'll know whether he's gone completely off the deep end and is out to get Marge simply because she's a friend of mine, or what.

A momentary look of surprise crossed Griggs's face as he came to the door and saw the three of them standing there.

"What do you mean by blackmailing Orin that way?" Marge snapped without preamble.

Griggs hesitated, and Shelbie could not help but wonder at the faint uncertainty she sensed in his manner. If there was one thing about C.G. you could always count on, it was his certainty. Except for a couple of minutes last night . . .

"Please," he said, "come in. I—I think I can explain."

"Explain?" Marge's voice was derisive now. "Sure, go ahead! I'd love to hear an explanation of what you did! And while you're at it, you can explain what you did to Shel, too!"

Griggs's eyes darted toward Shelbie, as if he had forgotten for the moment that she was there. "Oh yes, the job at Argos . . ." His voice trailed off, and Shelbie's leaden anger was being slowly supplanted by confusion. She was beginning to wonder if, even temporarily, C.G. might actually be changing. First last night, and now this . . .

"Yes," Griggs went on, his eyes drifting toward Shelbie, "perhaps I can. At least I can try."

"It better be good!" Marge said, but the harshness was beginning to fade from her voice.

"I—I can't guarantee anything, but . . ." Griggs hesitated

again, and his features seemed to firm themselves. "It would be better if I showed you," he said, his voice more businesslike now. "And then, if you still want to have your special edition of the *Bugle* printed, I won't stand in your way."

"Show us? Show us what?" Curiosity seemed to be getting the better of Marge. "And what does the *Bugle* have to do with Shel's job?"

"You'll have to see to understand. Particularly you, Mr. Decker," he added, looking toward Matt.

"Me?" Matt's frown grew deeper.

"Yes," Griggs said, his voice nearly back to normal now. "Your uncle's money enters into the picture, too, so you're just as involved as the others—perhaps more so."

"How does Ben Cunningham's money enter into this? What do you know about that?" Matt asked belligerently.

Griggs shook his head. "I'm sorry, but I've known all about the missing money for some time. I—I heard about it from Carla several weeks ago. I know she shouldn't have told anyone, but I'm afraid I pumped her unmercifully."

"Why?" Matt asked. "What's your interest in *that?*"

Again Griggs shook his head. "It's too hard to explain this way. The only way— I'll just have to show you. It's the only way. What I have to show you will explain everything."

He paused, and then reached slowly into his jacket pocket. "Part of it is here," he said slowly, quietly, "but not all, not nearly all."

As he was speaking, he withdrew his hand from his pocket and held it out, palm up.

Lying in his palm was the missing pewter figure.

CHAPTER 16

"*You* stole it?" Shelbie's eyes widened in surprise. "Why? How? *What* is going on?"

Griggs closed his eyes briefly, as if bracing himself. "How is easy enough," he said. "Keys to your museum—and to the rest of the building—aren't that hard to acquire."

"Keys to the— You mean you just walked in and took it?"

He nodded but said nothing.

"And that other time, a couple of weeks ago—that was you, too?"

He hesitated, but again he nodded.

"Just trying to keep an eye on me? Or trying to scare me? Or what? C.G., I don't understand *any* of this! And now *this* thing!" She waved a hand at the pewter figure still in his hand. "Why steal *that?*"

He shrugged, and a faint smile forced itself onto his face as he looked at Matt and then Shelbie. "Just call it a hunch," he said softly. "You do believe in hunches, don't you?"

For a long moment, there was silence. Marge looked as if she were about to speak, but she quieted as she glanced at the uneasy expressions on the faces of both Matt and Shelbie.

"You said you had something to show us—in addition to that thing—that would explain everything," Matt said finally. "Something that would even explain my uncle's suicide."

"I didn't—" Griggs began, then stopped and shrugged again. "I didn't say that, not precisely, but Ben Cunningham's suicide will be explained, yes."

"All right, we're waiting."

Griggs blinked, hesitated again. The touch of amusement that had shown in his face a minute before was gone. "Very well," he said. "But it isn't here. It's— Mr. Decker, do you have the keys to your uncle's house and grounds?"

"Yes, but—"

"Good. That is where the answers are."

Matt scowled suspiciously. "I didn't know you had ever been there. Or was this something else you 'heard' from Carla Schaeffer?"

"I have been there—but not with Carla."

"Then with whom? How? Did you know my uncle?"

Another hesitation, an uncharacteristic uncertainty in Griggs's eyes. "In a way, I knew him." Then Griggs drew himself up, taking advantage of his height to look down at everyone, including Matt. He stepped out onto the porch, and it was only now that Shelbie noticed his appearance. His hair was mussed, as if he had been sleeping. His shirt was rumpled and open at the neck, and his jacket seemed to hang loosely. It was not quite as startlingly out of character as his appearance had been last night, but still . . .

"Just come with me to the Cunningham house," he said, "and all your questions will be answered." He stood looking from one to the other for a moment, then turned and strode off the porch toward his Mercedes in the drive beside the house. "I'll meet you there," he said over his shoulder.

It was beginning to rain—just a few spattering drops—when the Checker pulled up at the gate to the Cunningham grounds. Griggs sat waiting in his own car while Matt unlocked the gate and led the way along the narrow drive to the house and parked in front of the garage. The rain was not yet heavy enough to penetrate the elms that interlaced above the drive or the oaks that shielded them as they walked to the front door.

The house itself loomed over them darkly, and as Matt worked the key in the lock, the eerily familiar feeling of uneasiness, the prickly sensation of unseen eyes watching from the darkness, swept over Shelbie with renewed strength. For a moment, the rattle of Matt's key in the lock fell silent, and in a brief, hooded glance, his eyes met Shelbie's. He felt it, too, she thought, just as he had felt it last night, and the chill clamped its fingers more tightly around her spine as the first drops of rain finally worked their way through the leaves and branches and spattered icily on her face.

But the feeling was different this time, more complex. In addition to the sensation of an unseen presence, there was something else, something even more intangible, more difficult to define. Before, there had simply been the ever-present desire to dart a look over her shoulder, the feeling that, if only she could look fast enough, she could see whatever it was. But now there was more. There was—

Suddenly, as the door to the house swung open and they all crowded inside, it came to her. There was now a nagging sense of menace. Before, the unseen, imaginary presence had simply been there, lurking in the background, neutral. The uneasiness and chills had all been the workings of her own mind, reacting to the mystery, to the unknown.

But now . . .

It was not simply a presence, but a malevolent presence, waiting somewhere in the darkness, waiting for her to come within reach . . .

"Matt—" she began, but before she could say more, she felt his hands grasping hers, and a moment later the lights came on. Griggs stood by the switch.

"I know," Matt said softly, in almost a whisper, and she saw that his own eyes were moving restlessly, seeking something that still could not be seen, even in the light.

"Well?" Marge was looking around challengingly. Obviously she was not affected by whatever it was that hovered over Shelbie and Matt. She looked at the dark green walls, at the living room through the arch on the left, at the closed sliding door on the right and the narrow stairway leading upward to the second floor. Finally she turned to face Griggs, who was still standing by the now-closed front door.

"Well?" she repeated. "What do you have to show us?"

Griggs stood silently for a moment, his eyes flickering toward Shelbie. His face was totally expressionless, but still there was a sense of tension, as if two opposite emotions were warring within him, but neither was able to come to the surface.

Abruptly, he strode past them, his eyes straight ahead, not looking down at any of them. "It's upstairs," he said, and his long legs took the stairs two steps at a time. The lights flared in the second-floor hallway as Marge started up, followed closely by Matt and Shelbie. Matt's hand gripped hers more tightly than ever. The presence—the aura of menace—was even stronger, but there was nothing they could do, short of turning and running. But certainly, Shelbie told herself, whatever it was, C.G. was nothing if not protective. He might get her fired from her job, he might keep her from getting another, but his purpose—he believed—was not to harm her, but to get her back. So certainly now, he would not allow—

Abruptly, at the top of the stairs, Shelbie stopped, her grip on Matt's hand tightening painfully. Marge was a few feet ahead, at the open door to the master bedroom. Griggs was standing beside the door, motioning her inside, but his eyes were on Shelbie.

Suddenly, she knew! There was no source for the knowledge, but she knew it was true!

"It's *him!*" she breathed, pulling back, but for once Matt's thoughts did not seem to have kept up with hers. The revelation had not yet come to him, she realized as his puzzled face turned sharply toward her. "It's C.G.!" she said, pulling back toward the stairs, but still Matt hesitated.

And Griggs was no longer in the hallway ahead of them. He was gone, and—

From somewhere came the sound of a drawer being yanked open, and only then did Matt's mind—his hunch or feeling or whatever—catch up with Shelbie's.

But then it was too late. As Matt sucked in his breath in startled realization, before he had time to spin about and start down the stairs with Shelbie, Griggs appeared in the hallway again, slamming the door behind him.

He said nothing, but he didn't have to. The gun in his hand said everything.

CHAPTER 17

It was impossible, and yet it was happening.

It was C.G.'s face that stared at Shelbie from behind the gun, and yet the face was alien and unfamiliar.

He stood back from the door to the bedroom, motioning with the gun for them to come forward. Slowly, they came.

The door to the bedroom opened, and Marge's harsh voice stumbled to a halt as she saw the gun.

"C.G.," Shelbie began as she and Matt approached him slowly, "I don't—"

Griggs shook his head sharply, nervously, and she fell silent. If only the "feeling" had been more specific, she thought, if only it had come through a little earlier, while they still had a chance to do something about it! And now it was gone. Or was it just that it had merged with reality? The menace was no longer vague and unseen but very solid and very real, no matter how unbelievable it might seem.

And the unseen presence . . .

No, she had been wrong. The feeling—the presence—was *not* gone. It still hovered in the background. The feelings that it generated were simply being drowned in the more immediate emotions of reality, but it was still there. But no longer was it tinged with the malevolence and danger that had suddenly become reality. No longer was it trying to warn them. Instead—

Shelbie blinked, not sure if the feeling now originated in her own mind or in whatever it was that hovered nearby, for it was a feeling that could have arisen from either source: sadness, or perhaps hopelessness.

Then they were inside the bedroom, being shepherded toward the nearly invisible sliding door on the far side. The drawer to a bedside table lay on the floor, and Shelbie could see that, at the rear of the drawer, was a separate compartment that could not be seen unless the drawer was pulled completely from the table.

"Is that where the gun was?" Matt asked, looking at the compartment. "How did you know?"

"I told you I had been here before," Griggs snapped, and the gun wavered for an instant. He touched the baseboard near the door lightly with his foot, and the door slid back silently. He reached inside and turned on the light. The single chair in the center of the tiny room stood as it had before, facing the empty alcove in the far wall.

"Inside!" Griggs said, his eyes darting nervously toward each of the three. "And you—Matthew Decker—" The name sounded strange, almost alien on Griggs's tongue. "You will press against the wall near the floor, there, in that corner." Griggs pointed with the gun. Beads of sweat, Shelbie noticed, were breaking out on Griggs's forehead, and he brushed his free hand across his eyes.

Matt kneeled down, his eyes not leaving the gun as he lowered himself. He looked toward where the gun was pointing. Experimentally, he pressed against the bare wall.

"Lower!" Griggs snapped. "About three inches up from the floor."

There was a faint click when Matt touched the wall again, and an instant later a section of the wall beneath the alcove slid soundlessly downward, vanishing into the floor.

Marge gasped as she saw what lay in the recess within the wall, but Shelbie and Matt, somehow, were not totally surprised.

Four of the pewter figures lay at the front of the recess. Behind them stood two ordinary-looking suitcases.

"Bring the four figures out here," Griggs said, "and one of the suitcases."

"What are *those* things doing in there?" Marge exclaimed, but Griggs waved her to silence with the gun.

"Bring them out here," he repeated, and Matt carefully obeyed.

"What's in the suitcases?" Matt asked as he set the figures and the suitcase on the floor next to the chair. "The missing money?"

Griggs nodded, but the gun didn't waver. He backed out of the doorway into the bedroom. "Bring them out here and put them on the bed," he said.

Moving warily, Matt obeyed, then stepped back toward the smaller room as Griggs motioned again with the gun.

"What are you going to do with us?" Matt asked.

For an instant, Griggs's face contorted in what appeared to be agony, but then the pain was gone, replaced by a faint, forced smile. "You," he said, his eyes directly on Matt, "are going to kill the other two, and then kill yourself. Just the way your uncle and all the others killed themselves, only a little more rapidly."

Matt swallowed audibly. "You mean you're going to make it look like I killed myself—after you murder the others."

Griggs nodded his head slightly and the smile faded. He brushed at the sweat that still beaded his forehead, and his eyes momentarily glazed, then recovered.

"This is not the way I intended it to be," he said, "even after you found out as much as you did. I intended something easier on all of us than this, but now I can only—"

"C.G.," Shelbie finally spoke, "do you know what you're saying? Do you—"

"I am *not* Carson Griggs!" he snapped, a mixture of anger and contempt plain in the tone. "There is no point in your pleading with *me* because *he* was in love with you, Miss Wilson!"

"Then who—" Marge began, but stopped as the gun swiveled toward her. "All right," she said then, in the quiet, soothing tone recommended for use with madmen, "whatever you say. But what *is* your name? And why are you—"

Again Griggs shook his head sharply, strands of dark hair

sliding across his moistened brow. "It makes no difference!" he snapped. "Not now!"

He's right, Shelbie thought abruptly. This *isn't* my ex-husband standing here. It's his body, but that's all. The mind belongs to—to what?

She glanced at the pewter figures that lay in a heap next to the suitcase on the bed. His mind belonged to those . . .

Just as the mind of Willy Brockman had belonged to them.

And the mind of Ben Cunningham, and the mind of Rebecca Emrick.

And the minds of how many others?

But was the possession complete? Was there no remnant of C.G. still lurking behind those eyes? Nothing at all? If not, then why, a corner of her mind asked, did he hesitate? Why did his eyes glaze momentarily when he talked of their deaths—of *her* death? Why did he seem to be struggling with himself every second?

Shelbie moved toward him, a slow and cautious step. The gun jerked in her direction, and Griggs faltered backward, halfway into the bedroom.

But he did not pull the trigger, though she could see the tendons on the back of his hand standing out like wires. His entire body seemed so tightly wound that a single touch could shatter it.

"C.G.," she said softly, trying to remember how they had spoken, how her voice had sounded at the beginning, "I know you can hear me. I know—"

Again the head shook violently, sending beads of sweat flying. "No!" The voice—Carson Griggs's voice—came from between clenched teeth. "I am not— He no longer has the power to interfere!"

Shelbie took another step, and as she did, out of the corner of her eye, she saw Matt moving slowly, almost imperceptibly forward.

"I know you can hear me, C.G.," she repeated in a whisper. "I know that, in your own mind, you never *meant* to harm me. Any more than *you* mean to harm me now . . ."

"No! You cannot— *I* am in control! You—" Griggs's left hand, as if divorced from the rest of his body, fumbled stiffly in his jacket pocket, and a moment later it brought out the pewter figure. For a moment, the fingers clenched around it until the knuckles turned white, but then, in a small, spasmodic motion, the hand threw the figure to the floor.

Griggs's startled eyes darted toward the sound, as if it were a total surprise to him, as if the hand which had thrown the figure from him was not a part of his body.

And in that baffled moment, Matt charged forward, his outstretched hand grasping at the gun.

Somehow, the gun did not fire. Even though, for seconds, Griggs managed to keep the gun trained on Shelbie despite Matt's struggles to force the arm upward, he did not squeeze the trigger.

Nor did he shift the gun toward Matt. Instead, he struggled with his free hand to hold Matt off, and his other arm seemed frozen, like a trembling steel rod. His face was drenched in sweat, his eyes wide and unblinking, staring directly at Shelbie, his lips curled back in a grimace of pain and terror.

Then, as abruptly as Matt had leaped forward, the resistance seemed to go out of Griggs. In an instant, his arm was bent upward, twisted harshly by the suddenly unopposed force that Matt had been applying.

The gun fired.

Whether it was intentional, whether it was a reflex by whatever occupied Griggs's mind, or whether it was the last remnant of Griggs himself, it was impossible to tell. For a moment, as the explosion literally filled the tiny room with its thunderous echoes, his eyes locked on Shelbie's, but whatever message lay within them, she could not read it. She could only watch dazedly, with a churning mixture of relief and anguish, as his eyes glazed and he collapsed to the floor.

Matt, a spattering of blood on the front of his jacket, stumbled backward, his own eyes and features blank.

Then, as Griggs's fingers relaxed, allowing the gun to slide from his hand and thump onto the floor, a soundless scream tore through Shelbie's mind.

But it was not simply a scream. It was the same feeling, the same sense of an unseen presence that had been hovering over her for days, periodically tugging and probing at her mind and at Matt's, but now it was amplified a thousand times. It was the difference between being touched lightly by a misty rain and being totally submerged in dark and freezing water. For a moment that seemed to stretch on forever, she was enveloped, smothered. The presence—the *being!*—was everywhere, screaming, clawing for a hold on life, knowing that if it allowed itself to be torn loose now, life was gone forever.

And the images, the sounds! The memories! It was as if, for one impossible moment, a million voices were shouting at her, a million faces and scenes clamoring for her attention, a million thoughts begging to be remembered.

And yet, in the midst of the terror, at the center of the tumultuous clamor to survive, there was a feeling of overwhelming relief, of coming at last to the end of an impossibly painful ordeal, an exile that could be ended in no other way . . .

And then it was over.

The presence that had surrounded Shelbie an instant before evaporated as quickly as it had descended on her. She was once again herself—and only herself.

Only then, as the terror and relief both flooded away like waves receding on a beach, sweeping everything with them, leaving her limp and exhausted, did she realize that, together with Matt, she had slumped to the floor and was sprawling, half-seated, her back pressed against the wall of the tiny room.

She blinked, letting the real world crowd around her again. She looked up from Griggs's crumpled form only a few feet away, at Marge's open-mouthed staring face.

Abruptly, Marge seemed to come to life. Her mouth snapped shut and she lunged forward, kneeling down by Shelbie's side.

"Are you all right, Shel?" Her voice was weak and shaking.

"I—I think so," Shelbie said, discovering that her own voice was even more unsteady. "But Matt—"

Still seated on the floor, her back still leaning against the wall, Shelbie turned to look at Matt. He was coming around, but more slowly than Shelbie had. Only now were his eyes clearing, the slack blankness going out of his features.

She reached over and put a hand on his. "Matt?"

He blinked again, shaking his head. "Shelbie? What—" Then his eyes fell on Griggs's body across the tiny room. He closed his eyes again, leaned his head back against the wall. After a long silence, his eyes opened slowly and he looked at Shelbie.

"It's gone," he said.

She nodded silently, knowing that he, too, had experienced the death of whatever it was that had lived in C.G.'s mind.

But *was* it dead? The bodies it had inhabited—or tried unsuccessfully to take over—had died before. Ben Cunningham had died. Carla Schaeffer had died. Willy Brockman had died. Rebecca Emrick had died. And yet the being had continued to live, to use whatever was concealed in the pewter figures to force itself into another host.

But those deaths had been different, something in her mind told her. Those times, death had been deliberate, either because the being was ready to move on to a new host or because it found it could not control the new mind as fully and as easily as it wished. And those deaths had been slow, allowing the being time to retreat, to return to the shell of its own body or to the mind of some other creature before—

For a moment, wondering where the thoughts had come from, she shivered. Could the being be returning, nudging her mind back into its own channels once again? But no, this time it was only a memory, an infinitesimal fragment of the torrent that had raged through her mind. Only a memory . . .

Then, unbidden, other memories bobbed to the surface. Memories of the Brockman house when it was new. Memories of the man who had, at the being's command, formed the pewter figures around the—the *things*. Memories of other lives, other worlds, other times. Memories of the lake as it was before there were houses or boats, when Indian villages dotted the shore and only the bravest of the brave dared approach the demon who called them to do his bidding, to raise the protective earthen shrine over him. Memories of the demon who called for new life each generation and struck down those who were drawn within reach but still somehow managed to resist. And, finally, memories of inexorably increasing anguish and guilt that could no longer be suppressed, a guilt that had finally fragmented the being's mind, driving it to grasp suicidally at any mind it could reach even as another part of that same mind was bent only on gaining yet another brief span of parasitic life. . . .

Abruptly, Shelbie was back in the present. Matt's hand tightened sharply on hers, and as she turned toward him, he frowned and his eyes darted about the room, searching.

A chill shot along her spine. It was over, she told herself again! It can't be starting again, it can't! I remember its death! I remember—

Hastily, Matt released her hand and scrambled unsteadily to his feet. One hand went into his jacket pocket, and a moment later he snatched it back out, shaking it violently.

"It's burning up!" His voice was not a shout but an awed whisper, and for a moment he stood silently, his scorched fingers forgotten.

A tendril of smoke began to rise from the pocket, and then Shelbie knew: The being and its possessions were inextricably linked. When the being itself was finally destroyed, the possessions must follow to their own destruction.

As Shelbie scrambled to her feet, Matt was tearing his jacket off, throwing it on the floor.

"What's happening?" Marge was looking from one to the other, dumbfounded. "What's going on *now?*"

"The others!" Shelbie said to Matt, barely hearing Marge's words. "Are they—"

She looked around, toward the four pewter figures on the bed by the suitcase. Smoke was already rising from the bedspread around them. And from the rug beneath the one that Griggs had thrown to the floor.

And all of them were softening, the demon faces flowing into featureless blobs.

Matt grabbed up his smoldering jacket, tried for a moment to wrap the melting figures in them, but saw almost immediately that it was hopeless. Open flames erupted around the growing grey pool on the bed as he stumbled backward, and then there was an explosion like a firecracker. Blobs of molten pewter were thrown in all directions. New flames erupted wherever a speck of grey touched.

They ran, Marge pausing only for the instant it took to snatch the suitcase from the flaming bed.

And as they ran, along the hall and down the stairs, a brief flash of light glared through the windows facing the lake. As they halted at the bottom of the stairs, Matt grabbing up the phone to call the fire department, the sound of a muffled explosion reached them.

"The Mound . . ." Shelbie breathed. Then, slowly, she moved to the window at the far end of the hall, facing the water. Across the lake, nearly a mile away, a tiny area of flame and smoke confirmed her words and her thoughts.

Now it was truly over. The demon and everything associated with it—except for the painful, lingering shards of memory—were gone.

The findings, officially, were that both the death and the fire were accidental, and no one disputed them openly, not even Marge. The explosion that had leveled the Mound was not mentioned except as an odd coincidence, just another example of the mindless modern vandalism and destruction that plagued even rural communities like Elwood these days. And, eventually, a ruling would probably be handed down through the courts establishing that the money in the suitcase that Marge had snatched up was part of what had vanished from Ben Cunningham's estate, at which time Marge would no doubt get a reward generous enough to keep the *Bugle* solvent for some time or to set her up in a new business altogether.

In the meantime, when a teaching job in Claymore opened

up a few weeks earlier than Matt had expected, he and Shelbie immediately made arrangements to move her to Claymore. As she and Matt left town late in the afternoon of moving day, though, they found themselves not following the highway but detouring along the narrow blacktop roads around the lake. Finally, without a conscious decision being made, they found themselves stopping along the southern edge of the swampy area and walking the two hundred yards back along the narrow path to where the Mound had been.

For a long time, they simply stood and looked. It was the first time either of them had been near the area since that night. The Mound was simply gone. What rubble there had been was scattered in all directions, and the trees and grass for fifty feet in all directions had been burned. Because of the rain, the fire had gone out quickly and not spread. Today, in mid-September, the sky was blue, the air still warm.

"Do you still remember?" Matt asked.

Shelbie nodded. "A little."

"Do you believe what you remember?"

For what seemed like a long time, she looked at the remnants of the burned grass, the scorched branches, then turned to look across the lake. It took her a moment to locate the remnants of the Cunningham house, hidden as it was by the trees.

"I don't know," she said finally. *"Something* happened. *Something* was behind what had been happening around Elwood for the past hundred or more years. And when C.G.—or whatever he had become—died . . . But you remember that better than I do. Don't you?"

He nodded. "But we've never—compared notes, so to speak."

A note of tension was evident in his voice as he spoke, the first nervousness he had displayed since—

Abruptly, Shelbie felt the tension herself. She had allowed her mind to slip back to that night, to touch the countless splinters and fragments of memory—painful, alien memories—and she was not yet ready for that. On that night, someone or something had died, and in the process of dying, it had clawed its way into her mind and into Matt's, and it had poured its own thoughts and memories into theirs. But the memories were still separate, still tinged with an alienness, an "aura" that warned her—warned them both—not to examine them too closely—at least not yet. Her mind—their minds—were not ready to accept what they might find if they looked too far beneath the surface at all the fragments of former lives and at the being itself. Despite the warmth, despite Matt's arm across her shoulders, she shivered as an image of the pewter face darted through her mind once again.

"No," she said finally, "we haven't compared notes—yet."

Matt said nothing, but she could see in his eyes that he understood, that he agreed.

"Someday," he said softly.

"Someday," she repeated, and slowly, with an odd combination of apprehension and anticipation not unlike the sort that jogged Shelbie's adrenaline when she was looking forward to exploring an abandoned house, they walked back toward the car. "Someday . . ."

Jean DeWeese has written several gothic and mystery novels and, under a slightly different name, a number of science fiction novels and short stories as well as some nonfiction.

Prior to all this, the author was a technical writer, doing programmed texts on computers, integrated circuits, and space navigation.